THE TEMPLETON CASE

THE TEMPLETON CASE

by

VICTOR L. WHITECHURCH

PUBLISHING NEW YORK
EDWARD J. CLODE, INC.

Contents

THE TEMPLETON CASE 2
   Contents 3
   CHAPTER I. Reginald Templeton Comes to Marsh Quay 4
   CHAPTER II. The Visit to the Opposite Shore 12
   CHAPTER III. A Terrible Discovery 15
   CHAPTER IV. What Canon Fittleworth Found on the "Firefly" 23
   CHAPTER V. Detective-Sergeant Colson Discovers Clues 34
   CHAPTER VI. Colson is Baffled 43
   CHAPTER VII. The Inquest 53
   CHAPTER VIII. Winnie Cotterill Pays a Visit to Frattenbury 62
   CHAPTER IX. The Cigar Band 72
   CHAPTER X. Harold Grayson is Detained 80
   CHAPTER XI. The Canon's Cigars 89
   CHAPTER XII. Fresh Evidence 99
   CHAPTER XIII. Isaac Moss Explains 108
   CHAPTER XIV. Reginald Templeton's Letter 120
   CHAPTER XV. Detective-Sergeant Colson's Deductions 127
   CHAPTER XVI. Mr. Proctor Upsets Matters 136
   CHAPTER XVII. New Theories 147
   CHAPTER XVIII. Sir James Perrivale's Story 157
   CHAPTER XIX. Colson Makes an Appointment 162
   CHAPTER XX. Colson's "Imagination" 167
   CHAPTER XXI. Final Solution of the Problem 176

CHAPTER I.
Reginald Templeton Comes to Marsh Quay

Tom Gale leaned heavily on the low bulwarks of the little schooner *Lucy*, his arms folded upon the aforesaid bulwarks, his short, black clay pipe in his mouth, and his eyes fixed on the flowing tide glittering in the sunlight of a clear October day.

Tom Gale had nothing whatever to do, and was doing it well, lounging and thinking, for the most part, about nothing at all. He combined the offices of crew and cook of the little coasting schooner that was moored at the head of Marsh Quay, waiting for a load of gravel that was delayed. That very morning word had been brought that the contractor would not be able to cart the gravel from the pit, about three miles away, down to Marsh Quay until the following Tuesday. This was Saturday, and the "captain" and "mate" had incontinently taken themselves off to their respective homes at Frattenbury, leaving Tom Gale in charge.

Tom Gale did not in the least mind having nothing to do beyond taking care of a vessel that nobody was likely to run away with. There was good beer to be had at the "Mariner's Arms," not a hundred yards away, and there was a nice snug bar parlour in the "Mariner's Arms," where the evenings might be spent in comfort—for there was no risk in deserting the vessel for an hour or two.

Marsh Quay was on one of the little estuaries of the sea that pierced into the southern country from the Channel. Two miles northward, the grey, tapering spire of the Cathedral of Frattenbury stood out against the background of Downs and blue sky. The estuary, which ran up within a mile of Frattenbury to the westward, was at Marsh Quay only about two hundred yards in width, but broadened out southward until a curve hid its course towards the open sea.

Marsh Quay, as its name implied, was a little quay jutting out into the estuary from the eastern shore. It was only about fifty yards long, but fairly broad, and contained sheds for storage on either side, except at the end, where it was quite open for a space, which formed room for a small vessel to be moored on either side, as well as one at its extremity.

The quay was reached by a straight road of about half a mile, which turned out of the main road to Frattenbury, and ended abruptly on the quay itself. As one approached by this road one passed a few cottages on either side, while, just before one came to the quay itself, there was a good-sized house on the right, and the "Mariner's Arms" on the left. The seaward wall of the little inn was washed at the base at spring tides, and the windows looked out over the estuary.

On the right-hand side of the quay, screened by the buildings on it, was an anchorage for vessels of small draught at low tide. A couple of little yachts were riding here, while, drawn up on the shore, were two or three flat-bottomed light canoes and some small boats. Most of these belonged to the "Mariner's Arms," and were for hire, Marsh Quay being quite a little resort at high tide in summer, when Frattenbury people came out to fish, or to sail in the estuary.

On the shore immediately opposite was a wood, coming right down to the water's edge, already turning golden yellow with autumn tints. Above the trees of this wood, a few hundred yards inland, could be seen the upper part of a house to which a boat, moored to the tiny jetty opposite, evidently belonged.

At low tide the estuary was a wide expanse of black mud, except for a narrow channel winding in the middle, and the little pool beside the quay, which formed the anchorage. The tide from the Channel outside came in with a strong current which rushed back at the turn. Boating was not particularly safe, and even if one were sailing a light draught yacht, one had to know the shallows well, while heavier vessels coming up or going down with the tide had to stick to the mid-channel, to avoid running on the mud.

The *Lucy* was moored at the end of the quay, her bows pointing southward. It was almost high tide, still coming in, with only the vestige of a breeze from the south-west. As Tom, Gale gazed vacantly over the sparkling waters, a speck of white appeared, coming into view round the bend. His seaman's interest was aroused. Slowly he stretched himself into an upright position, and shaded his eyes with his hand.

Presently he muttered to himself:

" 'Tain't the first time he's come up. Knows his way about, or he wouldn't ha' steered off the point there."

The speck of white grew more distinct, evolving into the mainsail, foresail, and jib of a small, cutter-rigged yacht. She was making little more than tide-way, her sails every now and then flapping as the breeze dropped.

Tom Gale took a look round. The water was flowing by more slowly, the floating bits of seaweed hardly moving now.

"Reckon he can't do it," he said. "There 'ent wind enough to bring him up against this tide and it's almost on the ebb now."

Even as he spoke, the foresail came down with a run, followed by the jib. Then the mainsail slowly descended.

"What's he up to?" said Tom Gale. "Don't seem to know his way about arter all. If he drops anchor there he'll drag for a certainty and get on the mud. Much better ha' slipped back to Langham on the tide. Ah—I see."

For the yacht suddenly began to forge ahead, while a faint succession of thudding sounds came over the water.

"One of them auxiliary oil engines, that's it."

Gathering speed, the yacht came up the estuary, stemming the outflowing tide. Tom Gale could see two men on her now, one steering and the other stowing the sails.

Presently she came up near the quay, slowing down a bit, and Tom Gale, looking down, could make out both men plainly. The one engaged in stowing the sails had moved forward and was getting the anchor ready. He was evidently a sailor, and wore dark blue trousers and a jersey, with a peaked cap on his head. The other was a man who looked about fifty years of age, with moustache and short, iron-grey beard. His face was much tanned by exposure to weather. He wore dark trousers, a short reefer jacket, and a yachtsman's cap was tilted on the back of his head. As he passed beneath the schooner he looked up, caught Tom's eye, and shouted:

"Plenty of room round the quay?"

"Plenty o' room, sir," answered Tom, "but stand out a bit to get round—it's runnin' a smart pace."

"I remember," the other shouted back, with the air of one who was familiar with the estuary.

Tom Gale slowly paced the deck of the schooner to get a better view aft. He watched the little craft draw up to her anchorage; she was a smart little boat, painted white, with a green line round her just below the bulwarks, and Tom's practised eye saw that she had been painted quite recently. Abaft the raised cabin was a well, in which the steersman sat and controlled the engine, and the entrance to this cabin the doors of which were open, was from this well. Forward was a forecastle, evidently providing just room for a solitary "crew."

Tom Gale watched her as she came to her anchorage. In this pool, cut off, as it were, by the side of the quay, the water was scarcely affected by the flow of the tide. There was a splash as the anchor was heaved overboard, a rattle of the chain, and the yacht slowly swung to her moorings.

The interest dwindled. Tom Gale pulled out a big silver watch. It was one o'clock.

"Time for a pint, I reckon," he murmured.

Slowly and heavily he climbed over the bulwarks and walked along the quay to the "Mariner's Arms." A stout, pleasant-looking, rosy-cheeked woman was standing behind the little bar, polishing glasses. To her he nodded with the air of an old acquaintance, kept up by frequent visitations.

"Gimme a pint, please, missus."

She drew it out of a big cask that stood on trestles behind the bar.

"Weather keeps fine."

"Ah—not much to grumble at," he replied as he counted out coppers. "Anyone in the parlour?"

"Only the gentleman that's staying here."

"Who's he?"

She shook her head.

"Dunno. An artist. Leastways, he does a bit o' paintin'—and fishin' too," she added. "Been with me nearly a week now. Nice quiet young man. Don't give no trouble."

"I'll have a look at 'im."

"Ah, do."

Tom Gale moved across the bar, opened a door, and passed into the parlour that overlooked the estuary. As has been said, the bar parlour of the "Mariner's Arms" was snug and cosy. Also it was in harmony with its name and surroundings. Five models of ships stood on the broad mantelpiece, and the pictures consisted of oleographs of the departure of Nelson from Portsmouth Hard on his last voyage, his death at Trafalgar, and three or four ocean liners, and a brigantine under full canvas sailing on an impossible blue sea. The furniture was homely but solid, and a comfortable settee stretched along one side of the room.

Seated near the window, his unfinished glass of beer on the table by his side, was a young man of about five and twenty, smoking a cigar. He was clean-shaven, with fair hair rather inclined to curl, a firm, strong mouth, and clear blue eyes. He was dressed in a loose knickerbocker suit, and was wearing a soft turned-down collar.

Tom Gale touched his cap, and then awkwardly removed it as he sat down and put his mug of beer on the table.

"Good afternoon, sir."

"Good afternoon."

Tom Gale took a long pull at his beer. He was a sociable man.

"Nice weather, sir."

"It is, very."

"Doin' a bit of fishing, Mrs. Yates tells me."

The young man flicked the ash off his cigar, and smiled.

"Trying to," he said, "but I haven't had any particular luck, so far."

Tom Gale thereupon waxed garrulous on the subject. He knew the estuary well and was up to all kinds of fishing dodges. From fishing the conversation turned to sailing, and from sailing narrowed down to the yacht that had just anchored.

"Did you see her, sir?"

"I was watching her just now, before you came in."

"Little beauty, I call her. I reckon she could give points to a few in a smart breeze. Looks to me like one o' they Cowes boats. Never seen her up here before, but the skipper knowed the way right enough. 'Tain't the first time he's run up to Marsh Quay, I'll 'low. Handled her just right."

"Well, *you* ought to know," said the other with a laugh.

"Ah—reckon I does. Though I ain't had no chance o' sailin' a beauty like that. Nice thing to have nothin' to do, and a craft like her to do it in. One o' these here rich chaps, I expects, what can afford to live in luxury and have their wine and whisky and cigars whenever they pleases."

The young man had just drawn out his case, and was selecting a fresh cigar as Tom was speaking. He held out his case with a laugh.

"Don't be jealous of his cigars," he said; "have one of mine, if you like 'em."

"Thank 'ee, sir. I don't mind if I do. Not that I often smokes one—don't get the chance."

He took out a knife, opened it, and was about to cut the cigar, then hesitated.

"I'll save it till to-morrow, if you don't mind, sir. I always reckon a cigar's a Sunday smoke."

"All right," said the other, as he removed the band from his own cigar and threw it in the grate. The fire was ready laid, but the weather was warm and it had not been lighted.

Tom Gale stowed away his cigar in his pocket, drained his mug, and glanced out of the window.

"Hallo!" he said, "they're coming ashore."

"Who?"

"Gentleman from the yacht—and his man."

From the window they could see the yacht. A little dinghy was coming ashore, pulled by the sailor. As the bows grated on the stones he sprang out, took a bundle from the boat, waited till the other had moved into his seat and taken the oars, and then shoved her off again.

"Skipper gone back to the yacht," said Tom, who was still watching. "T'other coming along for a drink—if I knows a sailor man rightly."

Five minutes later the said sailor man entered the parlour, a mug of beer in his hand.

"What cheer, mate! Good day, sir," as he caught sight of the other.

The two men of a trade quickly forgathered together, while the other quietly smoked his cigar and now and then put in a word.

"Stroke o' luck for me," said the newcomer, with all the open frankness of his calling. "I ain't been this way this three year or more. Got an old uncle living over at Frattenbury, and the skipper's given me the night off to go and see him. Got to get back early to-morrow to get his breakfast for him."

"What, does he sleep aboard?" asked Tom Gale.

"Always, ever since I've been with him, and that's gettin' on for three weeks now. Don't like hotels, he says. Ain't been used to 'em. Been livin' up country in Africa or somewhere—explorer cove, seemingly. Knows his way about."

"How long is he puttin' in here?"

"Three or four days, I reckon. Knows Frattenbury; got a relative there, I think."

"How about his dinner to-night?" asked the young man. "Is he seeing to it himself?"

"No, sir. Goin' to walk into Frattenbury presently and have it there, he says. Comin' back to-night."

"Got a soft job, ain't ye?" asked Tom Gale with a broad grin.

"'Tain't bad. But he's mighty particular."

"Where did you pick him up?"

"Why, he only landed at Plymouth a month ago; came straight on to Salcombe for yachtin'—mad on it. My governor there hired him the boat and picked me out to see to him. We've been runnin' along the coast, putting in at Dartmouth, Weymouth, and Poole. Left Ryde early this mornin', then the wind dropped. Ah, he ain't a bad sort, ain't Mr. Templeton."

And he buried his face in his mug, and then wiped his mouth with the back of his hand.

The young man leaned forward a little in his chair.

"Did you say his name was Templeton?" he asked.

"That's right, sir; Mr. Reginald Templeton. It's painted on one of his trunks."

"And he came from Africa?"

"That's correct sir."

"And he's staying here several days?"

"Yes, sir. Well, I must be off. Good afternoon, sir. Come into the bar and have one with me afore I go," he went on to Tom Gale.

The latter obeyed the call with ponderous alacrity. The young man remained smoking thoughtfully. Presently the landlady came in to clear away the mugs from the table.

"Lor' sir," she said, "ain't you goin' out paintin' this beautiful afternoon?"

He shook his head.

"I'm not in the mood," he said.

"Well, sir, why don't you try a bit o' fishin'? There's whitin' to be caught off the quay head when the tide's ebbin'. And you'd get a bit o' bait off of Harry Turner, the second cottage down the road. I know he's got some."

"No, thank you, Mrs. Yates, I'm going up to my room. I've some letters to write."

His bedroom was over the bar parlour. When he reached it he looked out of the window.

He took a pipe from his pocket, filled and lighted it. But he seemed to have forgotten his letters. Instead of writing, he sat by the window, carefully watching to see if Mr. Templeton came ashore.

CHAPTER II.
The Visit to the Opposite Shore

Tom Gale, with the comfortable sensation of the replenishment of his inner man with a double portion of his favourite beverage, went back on board the *Lucy* and resumed his attitude of leaning over the bulwarks and gazing upon the estuary. Only, this time, he was aft of the schooner instead of forward.

The tide had gone down rapidly, and great patches of slimy black mud were showing on either side of the central current. Opposite, just southward of the small landing-stage where the boat was moored, a stony patch ran out into the estuary, banking up the water on the northern side. This made it possible, except at extreme low water, to cross in a small boat from shore to shore without running on the mud.

As Tom Gale puffed at his short pipe he was attracted by a noise from the yacht. Looking towards it, he observed that Templeton was hauling the dinghy alongside.

"Goin' ashore," murmured Tom.

Templeton got into the dinghy, cast her off, took the oars, and began rowing across the estuary. To do this he had to head the boat diagonally upstream and to pull with all his might athwart the current. Slowly he crossed over, Tom Gale grunting approval, till he reached the little pool of comparatively calm water formed by the stony patch. Here he got out, took the anchor, hitched it round a big stone, and shoved off the boat to the full length of her painter. Then he walked briskly up the shore and disappeared into the wood—towards the house.

The young man watching from the window of the "Mariner's Arms" had seen Templeton cross over.

He put on his hat, came downstairs and strolled out on the quay. Then he stepped aboard the *Lucy*, and began to talk to Tom Gale.

Presently he asked, nonchalantly:

"Who lives in that house beyond the trees yonder?" pointing to the opposite shore.

Tom Gale, who had been up and down the estuary scores of times, and was a confirmed gossip, answered readily:

"Over there? Oh, he's a London chap. Name o' Moss—Isaac Moss. He's a Jew, so they say."

"Ont-of-the-way place, eh?"

"He only comes down for week-ends. That's his craft—yonder," and he nodded towards one of the little yachts lying near the newcomer. "Has to keep her over this side, but rows across when he wants her. She's stowed for the winter now, I reckon. Lord, *he* can't sail her, sir. Has a man to do it for him."

"What is he?"

"Dunno. Something up in London. Reg'lar Jew, sir. Come walkin' out from Frattenbury one Saturday I was here—his motor had gone wrong, and couldn't run in to fetch him. Asked me to pull him across when a smartish tide was runnin', and give me thruppence for it. Look—that's him," and he pointed to the other side, where two men were coming out of the wood to the shore. "T'other's the skipper comin' back I reckon."

Templeton, for it was he, drew the dinghy ashore, stepped into her, and began to row across. The other, a small man, stood on the shore, apparently still talking to him.

The young man, who had been sitting on the bulwarks, rose, left the schooner, and walked back to the inn. From the window he again took up his watch. This time he was successful. Templeton, having boarded his yacht for a few minutes, pulled himself ashore, dragged the dinghy a little way out of the water and made her painter fast to a stump of wood. Then he began walking briskly over the field path that led to Frattenbury.

By this time it was well on in the afternoon. The young man came down, had his tea, and then strolled out. For some time he stood at the entrance to the quay looking at the yacht. The latter was only about twenty yards from the shore, and he could clearly make out the name on her bows—the *Firefly*.

Later on Tom Gale found a little company assembled in the bar parlour, and spent a pleasant, and somewhat beery, evening. At ten o'clock Mrs. Yates gently but firmly turned them all out. The little group stood talking for a few minutes in the road, and then separated. The night was very dark, but Tom Gale was accustomed to dark nights at sea. Mechanically observant, he could make out the dim shape of the dinghy, already half afloat on the flowing tide, while the outline of the yacht, riding at anchor, was just discernible. There were no lights showing on it.

"Skipper ain't come back yet; he'll have a dark, lonesome kind o' walk from Frattenbury," he said to himself as he made his way along the quay. Arrived on board the *Lucy*, he dived into the forecastle, lighted a candle, closed the hatch—he liked fuggy surroundings—removed his jacket, guernsey and trousers, rolled into his bunk, blew out the light, and in a few minutes was sleeping the heavy sleep of the saturated.

The tide rippled up the estuary. The lights in the "Mariner's Arms" and the cluster of cottages went out. Marsh Quay and its surroundings were still and quiet in the calm autumn night.

CHAPTER III.
A Terrible Discovery

Jim Webb, "crew" of the yacht *Firefly*, came walking briskly over the fields from Frattenbury the next morning. In the clear autumn air he heard the Cathedral chimes strike the half-hour, and compared the time with his watch. Half-past seven. His skipper breakfasted at half-past eight, so there was plenty of time for him to prepare the meal with the help of the little oil-stove in his cuddy.

It was only a few minutes later when he reached Marsh Quay. Mrs. Yates, who was standing at the open door of the "Mariner's Arms," greeted him with a "Good morning," which he returned.

The tide was out and the yacht rode at anchor in calm water. Moored to her stern was her dinghy, and Webb had to get aboard.

Mrs. Yates, who was a good-natured woman, had come out of the inn and strolled down to where he was standing by the water's edge.

"You'll be getting your master's breakfast, I suppose," she said. "If you want any hot water, I've got a kettle on the fire."

"Thankee kindly, missis, but there's a stove abord. Tell you what, though, I'll have to borrow one of these punts. I suppose that'll be all right?"

"You're welcome. These here belong to me, and a nuisance they are at times. The boys will get playing about with them. Look here—they've been at it again, the young rascals! I know this one was tied up all right yesterday." And she pointed to one which was unsecured to a post. "Them boys are the plague of my life," she went on, as Webb dragged the little craft down to the water and shoved off.

She stood, arms akimbo, watching him as he paddled the few strokes that brought him to the yacht. As he clambered aboard he waved his hand to her, and at that moment he noticed behind her the young man who had been in the bar parlour the previous evening push a bicycle, with a stuffed holdall strapped to it, and go quickly riding away along the road.

Mrs. Yates still stood looking out over the great expanse of mud that characterised the estuary at low tide. It was a pleasant morning, and she had nothing particular to do just then.

Turning, she stopped for a minute or two to tighten the painter of one of the other boats, and then began to walk slowly back to her house. Suddenly she stopped. A hoarse cry rang out over the water behind her. Turning once more, she saw Webb frantically climbing from the yacht into the canoe, shouting incoherently as he did so.

She ran to the shore to meet him as he landed.

"What's the matter?"

"Him—Mr. Templeton!" he cried as he staggered ashore.

"What?"

"Dead!"

"*Dead?* What do you mean?"

"Yes—dead! I found him lying there in the cabin—on the floor."

"But—but—surely——"

"I tell you he's dead!" cried the man; "and what's more, he's been murdered!"

"Oh, my God!" ejaculated Mrs. Yates, sitting down on one of the posts. "What do you mean?"

"What I say. The cabin door was open, but I didn't take no notice o' that. He always sleeps with plenty o' fresh air about. At first I thought he'd tumbled out of his bunk and stunned himself—till I saw something else on the floor—blood it was, missis. Then I took a closer look at him, and saw he was stone dead! Lyin' on his face, he is—and the blood all round him."

"Where—whereabouts was he hurt?"

"I dunno; I never stayed to see. What be I to do, missis? This is a case for the police, and——"

"What's the matter? What is a case for the police?"

They turned quickly. Coming out of the garden gate of the house opposite the "Mariner's Arms" was a little elderly man, with a perfectly bald head and clean-shaven face, like an egg. He was dressed in a loose velveteen jacket and grey flannel trousers, and wore a gaudy pair of woollen slippers.

"What the matter?"

"Oh, Mr. Proctor!" almost screamed Mrs. Yates, "I'm so glad you've come. It's murder, sir!"

"Mr. Templeton, sir," cried Webb; "he's been done to death—over there—on the yacht. I've just found him——"

"Steady, my man, steady. Try and keep calm and tell me all about it. If it's what you say, there's no time to be lost."

Under the quieting influence of the old gentleman, Jim Webb retold his ghastly story; Mr. Proctor pursing up his little round mouth, nodding encouragingly and now and then helping him out with a word or a question. Then he took complete command of the case.

"Someone must go to Frattenbury at once and tell the police, and bring a doctor."

"There's the young man what's lodging with me—Mr. Grayson," exclaimed the landlady. "He's just ridin' his bicycle into Frattenbury."

"He's gone," said Webb. "I seen him go just as I was gettin' aboard."

"Gone!" cried Mrs. Yates, "and never said good-bye to me?"

"What," said Mr. Proctor, "is he leaving for good?"

"Yes, sir. All of a sudden like. Came down an hour earlier for his breakfast and asked for his bill. I couldn't make it out."

"Well, well," replied Mr. Proctor. "Time enough to talk about him later. My young great-nephew is staying with me, and he's got a bicycle. I'll send him into Frattenbury at once. He's a sharp lad. Phil," he cried, turning to the house, "Phil, come here at once. Look sharp."

A bright-looking boy of about fifteen came running up. Mr. Proctor gave him hasty instructions. "Ride as hard as you can," he said.

"Righto, uncle. I'll do it in ten minutes."

"Good boy. Now, my man are you quite certain your master is dead?"

"Yes, sir—there ain't no doubt about it."

"Um—all the same, I'll go and have a look. You can pull me out."

Mrs. Yates waited on the shore till he returned, shaking his head.

"There's no doubt about it, I'm afraid. We can't do any more. I haven't moved anything. Best let the police find things just as they are. You two come into my house and have something. You're both scared, that's what you are."

He took them in and gave them a brandy and soda each. When they came out again the news spread rapidly, and a group of men, women and children gathered on the shore and gazed at the yacht. Tom Gale came along the quay, munching the remains of his breakfast. Mr. Proctor nudged Jim Webb's arm just as the latter was about to tell the story to an expectant audience.

"If you'll take my advice, my man," he said, "you'll say nothing. Wait till the police come, and let them take the lead."

Jim Webb accordingly lighted his pipe and remained dumb, much to the annoyance of the little crowds, the members of which began to speculate upon what had happened, and finally determined, to their great satisfaction, that Webb himself had committed the murder and that Mr. Proctor was keeping an eye upon him till the police arrived to arrest him. One of them even suggested to the latter:

"Hadn't we better lock him up in Mrs. Yates's cellar, sir?"

"Lock who up?"

"Why, *him*," pointing a condemnatory thumb over his shoulder at the unconscious Webb.

"Lock yourself up for a silly fool," retorted Mr. Proctor contemptuously.

Presently a motor appeared dashing down the road. It was driven by the superintendent of the police. By his side was the doctor, and in the back seat a burly constable and a man in plain clothes. They all jumped out. Mr. Proctor, who was still in supreme command, addressed a few words to the superintendent.

"You've done quite right, sir—quite right," said the latter; "and now we'll get on with things at once."

The superintendent was a quiet, refined-looking man, with a big black moustache. The man in plain clothes was of slight build, clean shaven, alert, and with shrewd grey eyes.

"Now, sergeant," said the superintendent, "you and I will go aboard with the doctor." He went on, turning to the constable, "You stay here. We shall want you, my man" he added, addressing Jim Webb. "What's your name?"

"Webb, sir."

"Told you so," said the man who had been snubbed by Mr. Proctor. "They always confront 'em with their victims. Why don't he put the handcuffs on him?"

A boat was run down to the water, and Webb pulled them out to the yacht.

The cabin was small. Webb, at the command of the superintendent, stayed outside, while the three men squeezed their way in. It was just the ordinary saloon of a small yacht. There was a bunk on either side, with lockers beneath and a folding-table, fixed to the floor, ran half-way down the centre. Huddled up to the floor, on his face, was the body of Reginald Templeton.

The doctor went down on his knees by his side and made a careful investigation.

"Stabbed in the back," he said presently, "and whoever did it knew the right place—right through the heart, as far as I can see. He must have fallen just as he is, and died instantaneously."

"How long has he been dead?" asked the superintendent.

The doctor went on with his examination, and consulted his watch.

"Some hours," he replied. "Rigor mortis has begun to set in. I should say it might have been after midnight—probably before. I should like to make a complete examination later on. Can't we have him moved to the inn?"

"That will be best," replied the superintendent. "We'll see about that."

"There's a motor just come," said Webb from the deck.

"That's mine," said the doctor. "I told my man to follow us out. I'll get back now, but I'll be down again later in the morning. There's no more I can do at present."

"All right. Colson," went on the superintendent to the detective, "you'd like to stay aboard and investigate a bit?"

"Yes, sir. I want a good look round. And I prefer working alone."

The superintendent took a last searching glance round the cabin.

"Webb!"

"Yes, sir?"

Webb put his head in at the doorway.

"That lamp," and he pointed to an oil-lamp swinging from the ceiling. "It's burning. Did you light it when you came aboard?"

"No, sir. I never noticed it."

"Very well. Now pull me ashore, please."

"Mr. Proctor," he said when he came ashore and the doctor had departed, "may we go into your house? I want to ask Webb some questions."

"By all means, Superintendent. Come along in. Have you had breakfast yet?"

"Yes, thanks."

"How about you, Webb?"

"I had some at Frattenbury, sir."

"Well, I'll leave you," said Mr. Proctor as he took them into his dining-room.

"Don't do that," said the superintendent. "You may be able to help us. Now then, Webb," and he took out his notebook.

"Yes, sir."

"Where's your home?"

"Thirty-one, Fore Street, Salcombe, sir."

"You're a sailor?"

"I work for Mr. Jefferies, sir. He lets out boats. He hired the *Firefly* to Mr. Templeton—Mr. Reginald Templeton, sir."

"When?"

"Three weeks ago."

"You've been with him ever since?"

"Yes, sir," and he recapitulated what he had told Tom Gale in the inn parlour.

"Who was Mr. Templeton?"

"He'd just come from Africa, sir. I reckon, from what he said, he'd been exploring or something. But he didn't talk much. He knew how to handle a boat, sir."

"I see. And you visited all these places?"

"Yes."

"Do you know if he had any particular reason for coming here?"

"I think he had, sir."

"Why?"

"He asked from the first whether I knew the coast. I said I did. I've an uncle in Frattenbury, sir. And I've sailed in these parts several times. He seemed pleased when I told him this."

"Anything else?"

Webb thought a moment.

"He mentioned he'd be here some days, sir. Said he had business. Said he was expected."

"Who by?"

"I can't say, sir. Only——"

"Yes?"

"When we was in Weymouth he gave me a letter to post—and, well——"

"You read the address?"

"Well, yes, sir."

"Very well. What was it?"

"To a parson in Frattenbury, sir. A reverend gentleman, name of Fittlemore—or something like that."

"Fittleworth?" asked the superintendent sharply.

"That's it, sir; Fittleworth was the name."

"Canon Fittleworth," said the other. "Well, that's a help, anyhow. Now tell me about last night."

Webb told him how he had had leave to stay in Frattenbury, and that Templeton had mentioned he was going to dine there. A few more questions, and the superintendent glanced over his notes.

"Well," he said, "there'll be an inquest, of course, and we shall want you, Webb. What are you thinking of doing?"

Webb hesitated.

"I don't much fancy sleeping alone on the *Firefly*, sir. I could get a bed at the inn here, or my uncle at Frattenbury will put me up."

"All right, so long as you keep in touch with us. That's all for the present. Thank you very much, Mr. Proctor. You can go, Webb."

Mr. Proctor rose from his chair, crossed the room and showed Webb out of the door. Then he took down a box from the shelf.

"Can I offer you a cigar, Superintendent?"

"Thanks very much." The policeman lighted his cigar, looked over his notes for a few minutes, and then said: "You're a good judge of cigars, Mr. Proctor."

"I am," replied the little man with a smile. "This is a strange case."

"Um," said the superintendent. "It's too early to form an opinion yet. But one thing is fairly obvious. Whoever murdered Mr. Templeton must have known he was coming here and must have got out to that yacht after he returned from Frattenbury and was aboard her."

Mr. Proctor flicked the ash from the cigar he was smoking, and observed dryly:

"Or have got aboard first, and waited for him there."

"What makes you say that?" asked the superintendent, looking up quickly.

"Only because it's just as obvious as your own theory. I thought it might be worth considering."

The superintendent reflected for a minute.

"Yes—it is," he admitted. "Now I must be going. I shall be back shortly."

Before he finally left for Frattenbury he pulled out to the *Firefly* and had a few words with the detective-sergeant.

"When you've finished here," he said, "you'd better make a few inquiries on shore. Find out who owns the boats about here. One of them must have been used by the murderer, otherwise the dinghy wouldn't have been here. Get to work among the people, and make a note of them, or of any strangers. I'm off to see the coroner. Also I've discovered that Templeton was probably dining with Canon Fittleworth last night. At any rate, he knew him. I'll bring the Canon back with me if he's able to come."

"Right, sir. I'll do what I can."

After a last injunction to the constable on the shore, the superintendent entered his motor and drove off.

"He ain't took that 'ere man back with him, after all," said the disappointed spectator who had fixed the crime onto the unfortunate Jim Webb. "And that's what we pays our police for!"

CHAPTER IV.
What Canon Fittleworth Found on the "Firefly"

Canon Fittleworth had only just returned to his house in the Close from the early Sunday service in the Cathedral, and had sat down to his breakfast with his wife and daughter. He was a cheerful-looking ecclesiastic, apparently midway between forty and fifty, wearing pince-nez over a pair of keen brown eyes.

He had just answered a question put by his daughter, and was beginning to attack his egg, when a servant came in.

"If you please, sir, Superintendent Norton wishes to speak to you. He says it's very particular. I've shown him into the study, sir."

"The police!" exclaimed Doris Fittleworth. "What have you been doing, father?"

"I've quite a clear conscience, dear. Tell him to wait ten minutes," he added to the servant.

"Please, sir, he said he must see you at once," she replied.

"Oh, very well," said the Canon, not pleased to be interrupted at his meal. "Keep my toast warm," he added to his wife as he went out of the room.

"Good morning, Superintendent. You wanted to see me!"

"Good morning, sir. I'm sorry to disturb you, but it's urgent."

"Anything wrong?"

"I'm afraid so. Will you tell me, please—do you know a Mr. Reginald Templeton, and have you seen him lately?"

"Why, of course I do. He's my cousin. He was only dining with me last evening. I hadn't seen him for a long time. What is it?"

"I'm very sorry to tell you, Canon, that Mr. Templeton was discovered on his yacht at Marsh Quay this morning, dead."

"Dead? Why, he was in the best of health last night!"

"Murdered," went on the inspector gravely.

The Canon started, and seized both arms of the chair in which he was seated.

"Good heavens!" he exclaimed. "This is terrible, Superintendent. Reginald *murdered*, you say?"

Briefly the superintendent gave him the details, explaining how he had ascertained that the Canon knew the murdered man.

"Exactly. He wrote to me from Weymouth, and again from Ryde. I was expecting him last night. I hadn't seen him for six or seven years—he'd been abroad. I wanted him to stay the night, but he wouldn't. He was always keen on boating, and was enjoying the life, he told me. Would to heaven he *had* stayed!"

"What time did he leave you?"

"He got here between five and six. We dined early—at seven. He left about half-past eight."

"Going straight back to Marsh Quay, I suppose?"

The superintendent had taken out his notebook.

"No, he said he had a call to pay first in Frattenbury."

"On whom?" asked the other, keenly interested.

"He didn't say. He was a very reticent man—always. I wondered at the time, because I didn't remember that he knew anyone here besides ourselves."

"I thought perhaps, Canon, you would like to see him—in fact, I should wish you to, if you can. I have to see the coroner, then—in about a quarter of an hour—I can come back and run you down in my car."

"By all means," replied the Canon. "I'll come if you think I can be of any use."

"Thank you, Canon, I'm sure it will help us."

He went out, and the Canon returned to break the terrible news to his family.

The superintendent drove a little way through the ancient city to a quiet, Georgian street, and stopped before a solid, square-looking house, which bore a brass plate on the door with the inscription, "Mr. F. Norwood, Solicitor." A minute later he was in the presence of Mr. Norwood, who rose from his chair to greet him.

Mr. Francis Norwood was one of the best-known professional men in Frattenbury and its neighbourhood. He had a large and select practice, an old-established one inherited from his father. He was an austere-looking man, with a hatchet-shaped face, large nose, thin, tightly-compressed lips, and old-fashioned mutton-chop whiskers. His hair, which was inclined to be grey, was thin and carefully parted in the middle. He wore dark trousers, a black cutaway coat, and black tie with a small gold pin.

He looked the very epitome of a dry, respectable lawyer, and eminently suitable for the environment of a cathedral city. He had never married—people said unkind things about him in this respect—that no woman would accept such a dry stick of a man—that he was too fond of himself and too close with his money to risk a partner.

For many years he had held the office of coroner—as his father had done before him. Many people called him selfish in still holding it. There were younger and struggling men who would have been glad of the occasional fees, whereas Francis Norwood was reputed wealthy. But this criticism—even if he knew it—had no effect upon the staid lawyer. He stuck to his post and he stuck to the fees which it brought him.

"Good morning, Superintendent; won't you sit down?" said the lawyer, motioning the other to a chair, and reseating himself. "What is it?"

"A case of murder, I'm afraid, Mr. Norwood."

"Murder? Dear, dear! That's very serious. Tell me about it."

As the superintendent told his story, the coroner sat bolt upright, listening intently, his elbows on the arms of his chair, the tips of his fingers pressed together.

"Yes," he said, as the other finished, "a bad case—a very bad case. I'll open the inquiry to-morrow. We shall have to adjourn it, of course. Let me see"—and he consulted a pocket diary. "Two o'clock to-morrow. Will that do?"

"Quite well, Mr. Norwood. It will give us time to get the preliminary facts in order."

"Just so. As far as my recollection serves me, there is a public-house close to the quay?"

"The 'Mariner's Arms,'"

"Ah, just so. The inquest will take place there. You will summon a jury?"

"Certainly."

The coroner folded his hands again. He was an extremely stiff individual.

"This will mean a lot of work for you," he said. "Have you any clue so far?"

"There's been no time yet, Mr. Norwood. I left the very best man we've got at Marsh Quay—Detective-Sergeant Colson, an extremely smart fellow."

"I see. Exactly. Do you intend to call in the services of Scotland Yard?"

The superintendent smiled.

"That depends on what the Chief Constable says, Mr. Norwood—when I've made my report to him. But we like, if we can, to get the credit of a case like this ourselves. And I've great confidence in Colson. However, developments will probably answer your question."

"Exactly. It's no affair of mine of course. But I hope you'll take every step to find the murderer."

"You can trust us for that," replied the other as he rose to go. "Two o'clock to-morrow, then?"

"Two o'clock to-morrow, Superintendent," repeated the coroner. "I'll be there."

He accompanied the policeman out of the room and through a big square, stone-paved hall to the front door, shaking hands with him stiffly and limply as he left.

A few minutes later, the superintendent was driving Canon Fittleworth to Marsh Quay. As they reached the spot, he pointed out the *Firefly*.

"Dear me," said the Canon, "we were to have come over for a sail in her to-morrow. How terribly sad!"

When they arrived on the yacht they found Colson sitting on deck, smoking. He hardly looked at them. The superintendent, who knew his man, took the Canon into the little saloon. The body had been laid on the table ready for removal; a handkerchief was over the face.

Canon Fittleworth lifted it reverently.

"Poor fellow!" he exclaimed; "it's Reginald Templeton, of course—poor fellow!"

He was almost breaking down. The superintendent, a sympathetic and sensitive man himself, said:

"I'm going to speak to Colson, sir."

The other nodded. When he was alone he kneeled down, bowed his head, and prayed silently for a few minutes. Then, without rising, he looked about him mechanically.

At times of great stress the smallest objects are often noticeable. An instance of this strange truth occurred just then. The Canon's gaze fell on something lying on the floor of the cabin—partly bright red and partly shining. With a sort of muffled curiosity, he stooped and picked it up. It was a cigar band.

Now there is nothing particularly striking in a cigar band. It is a common enough object. True, cigar bands vary in their queer little heraldic designs and miniature shields, and inscriptions of the firms that produced them, in Spanish. But, as the Canon looked at that torn object, he suddenly started.

"That's queer," he murmured, smoothing it out and regarding it intently. He took off his glasses, wiped them with his handkerchief, and had another look. His brow puckered. Again he said:

"Queer—very queer."

Now the Canon was entirely ignorant of police methods—they had never come within his sphere. Also, by virtue of his office and dignity, he was accustomed to act on his own initiative. Besides, that particular cigar band had led his thoughts far away from that scene of death—it was something personal that was arresting his attention. Also, he had been, all his life, one of those men who are reticent up to a point, that point being the exact moment when they are ready to lay all their cards on the table. He wanted to compare this particular bit of red and gold with something else before he could be quite certain of the matter that was agitating his mind.

These several reasons combined to prevent him doing what many a man would have done under similar circumstances—calling in the superintendent. It never entered his head at that moment that he ought to do any such thing. Instead, he took out a his pocket-case and carefully deposited the cigar band within it.

Then he rose from his knees and looked round the cabin, gazed again at the cold, white face on the table, spread the handkerchief over it, and slowly left the saloon—a great weight on his mind as the thought of his murdered cousin pressed itself uppermost. In silence he rejoined the two policemen on the deck, took his seat in the boat, and came ashore with them. For the time being the incident of the cigar band had passed out of his mind.

Mr. Proctor greeted them.

"Canon Fittleworth, I presume?" he asked politely. "My name is Proctor. May I be allowed to express my sympathy, sir? I understand the unfortunate gentleman is a relative of yours."

"Thank you very much."

"And may I venture to ask you both to come in and have a glass of sherry and a biscuit? I'm sure you both need something after such a strain. It will give me much pleasure if you will."

"It's very good of you," said the Canon. "And I won't refuse."

The little man took them into a cosy dining-room which overlooked the estuary. On the table was a plate of sandwiches, biscuits, a decanter of wine and glasses. He helped them to refreshments and then said:

"If you'll excuse me—pray make yourselves at home."

"Thank you," said the superintendent as Mr. Proctor left the room. He did not press him to stay, as he wanted a few minutes' conversation with Canon Fittleworth.

"We shall have to ask you to give formal evidence of identification at the inquest to-morrow, Canon. And, of course, you will tell the jury what you know of Mr. Templeton—and his movements last evening."

"Certainly. Though, as a matter of fact, I know very little of him. As I told you, he has been abroad for some years. He's a bachelor—and was always a rolling stone. He told us something of his travels last night—not very much."

The superintendent nodded. "There are one or two questions I want to ask, please."

"By all means."

"Tell me—do you think Mr. Templeton had any object in coming to Marsh Quay other than paying you a visit?"

"Yes," answered the Canon, "I feel sure he had. He spoke vaguely of having business in the neighbourhood—but I haven't the slightest idea what it was—except, yes—now I come to think of it he did drop a hint."

"What was it?" asked the superintendent, leaning forward.

"He said that ever since he landed in Plymouth he'd been carrying about something valuable that made him a bit anxious—that he was glad to be getting rid of."

"Did he say what it was?"

"No. He only mentioned it casually."

"H'm," mused the other, "there may be something in this. It may mean the motive for the crime—robbery."

"That is quite possible. I wish he'd told us more."

"Exactly. One other question. You say he was going to see someone in Frattenbury last evening——"

"Yes—but I haven't the slightest idea who it was."

"I know—but I was going to ask, did he give you a hint of anyone else he knew in this neighbourhood?"

The Canon thought carefully before he replied:

"Only that, as I said, he referred to some business that he had in hand here."

The superintendent was silent. He drank his glass of wine and looked out of the window. Colson was coming up the garden path. In a few seconds he entered the room.

"There's something I must tell you at once, sir." And he looked at the Canon.

"Go on," said the superintendent. "We are speaking in confidence," he added.

"Certainly," said the Canon.

"I've just been talking to a man named Gale who was here all day yesterday. He saw the *Firefly* come in and anchor, and what's more he saw Templeton row himself across to the other side—yonder," and he pointed out of the window, "and reappear after about three-quarters of an hour with a Jew named Moss, who lives in that house you can see above the trees. He recognised him distinctly, even at that distance. Then Templeton pulled himself back to the yacht—and afterwards came ashore here."

"Good!" exclaimed the superintendent, springing to his feet. "We'll interview this man Moss at once."

"I should like to come too, if I may," said Canon Fittleworth.

"There's no reason why you shouldn't. Ah—Webb is about still. We'll get him to row us across. Come along, Colson."

Arrived on the other side of the estuary, they made their way through the woody path and in a few minutes came out on an open space where the house was standing. It was a modern two-storied villa, with a small garden and a garage.

The superintendent rang the front door bell. The door was opened by a woman of about five and thirty. Her face paled a little as she saw the police uniform.

"Does Mr. Moss live here?"

"Yes, sir—when he's down here for week-ends."

"Is he in?"

"No, sir."

"Do you know where we can find him?"

"He's gone back to London, sir, with Mrs. Moss."

"Gone back to London, when?"

"This morning, sir—by the early train from Frattenbury. My husband motored them both into Frattenbury."

"Do you live here with your husband?"

"Yes, sir. We're caretakers all the week. I do the cooking, and Mrs. Moss brings down a maid when they come for week-ends."

"Is your husband in?"

"Yes, sir—I hope there's nothing the matter?"

"Nothing for you to disturb yourself about. Will you call your husband, please, and come back yourself."

The man who appeared was a little defiant, but the superintendent cautioned him sharply, and he answered the questions he put—though rather sullenly.

"You drove your master and mistress into Frattenbury this morning?"

"Yes—I did."

"At what time?"

"To catch the 7.35 up train."

"When did you get the order—last night?"

"No—this morning."

"It must have been very early?"

"Soon after six o'clock."

"Do they often go up by this Sunday morning train?"

"No, sir—I never knew them do it before. It's generally on Mondays they leave—or, leastways, Mr. Moss always does."

"Do either of you know where he lives in London?"

"Not his private house, sir—we forward any letters that come—or write to him at his business address."

"And what's that?"

"13a, Hatton Garden, sir."

The superintendent and Colson exchanged significant glances.

"That seems to point out what his trade is," said the latter.

The superintendent nodded, then he went on with his questions.

"Did your master receive any visitor yesterday afternoon? Now, be careful, please."

The woman shot a glance at her husband—who only stared stonily back, with his hands in his pockets.

"I—I didn't let anyone in, sir."

"Oh, you didn't. But you saw someone?—you must tell me, please."

"I—I happened to be looking out of the window, sir—and Mr. Moss was sitting on a chair on the lawn—with another gentleman."

"What was he like?"

"I couldn't say, sir. I didn't notice him particularly. And he had his back to me."

"Very well. What time was this?"

"Somewhere between four and five, sir."

"Anything else?"

"Mr. Moss must have brought him indoors, sir. I heard them talking in his study, as I came by, but I never saw him."

"Did you hear anything they said?"

"No, sir—I should scorn to listen."

The superintendent thought for a moment, then he said:

"Thank you—that's all."

The man stepped forward.

"I should like to know if there's any trouble about, sir. We're decent folk, my wife and I, and we don't want to be mixed up in no rows—especially if the police are in it."

"That's all right, my man—don't worry. We only wanted to see your master about this visitor of his. Another time will do very well. Good day."

As they walked back to the boat, the Canon remarked:

"We don't seem to have got very much information here."

"No, but it's important," replied the superintendent, "and we've got to find out why this Mr. Moss left in such a hurry. We'll very soon get onto his track."

Colson nodded thoughtfully, but said nothing. He was a silent man when at his work—except when he was drawing out information. Then he could be companionable enough. But he rarely made remarks as to probable or possible results while he was actually investigating a case.

When they came back to Marsh Quay, Colson was left in charge, and the constable instructed to warn men for the jury. The body had been carried over to the "Mariner's Arms" and laid on a bed in one of Mrs. Yates's rooms. The superintendent drove Canon Fittleworth back to Frattenbury, and then went on to report to Major Renshaw, the Chief Constable, who lived just outside the city.

That evening, Canon Fittleworth sat in his comfortable study, discussing the events of the day with his wife and daughter. He put his hand in his pocket for something, and felt his case there. Then he remembered.

"Oh!" he said, "that reminds me."

"What, dear?" asked his wife.

"Wait a minute."

He got up, unlocked a cabinet, and took out a box of cigars. Then he produced the red and gold band from his pocket, and carefully compared it with those on the cigars in the box.

"Look here," he said, as he went back to his seat; "I found this lying on the floor in the cabin where poor Reginald was murdered."

"Poor man," said his daughter, as she took the cigar band to look at it; "do you think that he was smoking when he was murdered?"

"No," said the Canon; "Reginald did not smoke. I offered him a cigar last night and he refused it. He said he hadn't smoked for years, and he disliked it."

"Oh, daddy," exclaimed the girl, "you ought to have shown this to the police!"

"I suppose I ought—yes—I never thought of it. However, I shall bring it forward at the inquest to-morrow. But there's something very queer about it," he went on.

"What is it, Charles?" asked his wife.

"Why, it's off one of my own cigars!"

"Off one of your own cigars?" exclaimed his daughter.

"Look for yourself," and he passed the box over to them.

"But," said the girl, when they had both compared the band with the others, "anyone might smoke the same sort of cigar."

"No, they mightn't. That's just the point," replied the Canon dryly. "This box was sent to me by my Spanish friend, De Garcia—you remember him? Well, he wrote to say they are a special brand reserved for the planters. They never sell them anywhere. What do you think of *that*?"

CHAPTER V.
Detective-Sergeant Colson Discovers Clues

"Mrs. Yates," said Detective-Sergeant Colson, as he finished a modest meal, served at his request in the "Mariner's Arms," "I am thinking of making my quarters here, at all events till the inquest is over. Can I have a room?"

"I'm only too glad to have you, sir," replied the buxom landlady. "I'm not much given to be afraid, but I don't like the idea of being alone in the house with a corpse, and I was thinking of asking a neighbour to sleep here."

"You're a widow, aren't you?"

"Yes, sir—these six years."

"Well, I'll be here to-night. I'm going into Frattenbury presently, and shall cycle out, probably a bit late."

"You can have the room Mr. Grayson had, sir. It's a pleasant one, above this, looking out over the water."

"Who is Mr. Grayson?" he asked.

"A young gentleman—an artist—who's been lodging here nearly a week. He left early this morning."

"Oh, did he?" said the detective, lighting his pipe. "This seems a rare place for people leaving early on Sunday mornings."

"Eh, sir?"

"Oh, never mind. Tell me about this lodger of yours. What time did he go away?"

"It was just before the murder was discovered, sir. He came downstairs early this morning, and said would I get him some breakfast because he'd suddenly changed his plans and was going away. Seemed strange, didn't it, sir? A nice, quiet young gentleman he was, too."

"How did he go?"

"On his bicycle, sir—same as he came here. Oh, he was a perfect gentleman, never gave me trouble, and paid up all right."

The detective had taken out his notebook.

"I wish you'd give me a description of this young man, Mrs. Yates," he said.

"Oh, Mr. Colson, sir," she exclaimed, "you don't mean to say as how you think 'twas him as done it?"

The detective laughed.

"Come, come, Mrs. Yates," he said; "I never said it was so bad as that. But, you see, we policemen like to know about all the people that were near a crime. That's why I'm asking you to help me. The smallest evidence may be valuable, and this young man may have noticed something yesterday. You see, he left before the murder was discovered, so he couldn't know we wanted him, could he?"

Mrs. Yates, all suspicions removed by Colson's bland manner, gave him, so far as she could remember, a description of her lodger, which the detective carefully took down. When she had finished, he said:

"Thank you, Mrs. Yates; excellent! You really ought to belong to the force, you remember everything so well. Observation is a very great gift, and you've got it. Splendid!"

Mrs. Yates smiled a smile of satisfaction. She was not proof against flattery. The detective saw he had scored a point.

"Now I'm going to take you into my confidence," he went on blandly. "I'll let you into a little secret. We detectives aren't half as clever as people think we are, and I don't mind telling you—quite between ourselves, you know—that this is going to be a difficult case. You wouldn't think it, perhaps, but, up to the present moment, I haven't the slightest idea as to who committed the murder."

Mrs. Yates had sat down in a chair and was regarding him fixedly, taking it all in.

"Lor' sir," she exclaimed, "you don't say so?"

He nodded gravely.

"It's quite true," he said, "and I want you to help me."

"Me, sir? What can I do?"

"You're a discreet woman, Mrs. Yates—a very sensible woman. And I'm sure you can hold your tongue if you like."

"I never was one to gossip."

"I knew it! Well, now, when I come back this evening I don't want anyone to know I'm here. You put some supper up in my room—show me now how I can get up to it without being seen—and if anyone asks where I am, you can tell them the truth, that I'm gone into Frattenbury, see?"

Mrs. Yates, who was almost trembling with excitement, showed him how he could get in by a back door she would leave unlatched. She also showed him a shed where he could put his bicycle.

"And one other thing, Mrs. Yates," he said; "you're going to keep your mouth shut, but you must keep your ears open. You're sure to have men in to-night discussing the murder. If you hear them say anything about having seen Mr. Templeton—or any strangers about—you make a note of it and let me know."

"I will, sir. I'll do what I can."

Colson took his hat and stick and a dispatch-case which he had brought over in the morning.

When he got outside the inn he walked over to Constable Gadsden, who was still on the spot. Quite a number of people were about, for the news had spread rapidly, and anything so gruesome as the central scene of a murder is attractive.

"Well, Gadsden," said he, drawing him to one side, "you haven't let anyone go on board the yacht—no newspaper men, or anyone?"

The burly policeman grinned.

"Trust me for that, sergeant."

"Mind you don't. I'm going into Frattenbury now. I'll send a man out to relieve you."

"Thank you, sergeant. I've found out something since I saw you."

"What?"

The policeman opened his pocket-book. No self-respecting constable ever reports to a superior officer without a reference to this mysterious compendium.

"Man o' the name o' Simmonds—George Simmonds—lives in the cottage yonder—states that he was walking along the field path yesterday and met a man of the description o' Mr. Templeton going into Frattenbury—between half-past five and six."

"May be useful," replied the detective. "More useful still, though, if he'd seen him coming back. If there's anything else to report you can do so to the superintendent when you get back to Frattenbury."

He himself took the field path to Frattenbury, and not the road. For half a mile or so the path ran by the side of the estuary, separated from the shore by a low hedge. Then, just as one got over a stile, it turned abruptly and led through a series of marshy meadows. There had been rain a few days before, and in places the path was damp, showing a number of footprints.

Just by one of the stiles was a particularly impressionable bit of ground. The stile had a high step, from which one naturally jumped and left well-defined footprints. Colson seated himself on the stile, opened his dispatch-case, and drew out a shoe. Then he got down into the path and investigated all the footprints narrowly, testing them by measuring them and comparing the results with the shoe.

Presently he gave a little grunt of satisfaction. The shoe exactly fitted one of the footprints. Walking slowly on, he was easily able to trace these particular footprints going towards Frattenbury.

"Doesn't help much," he said to himself, "but—ah, here's what I want."

For he caught sight of a similar footprint—and then another—pointing in the reverse direction. Several more were apparent as he walked on.

"That settles it," he exclaimed; "Templeton walked back to Marsh Quay by the same route. I'm glad I thought to bring one of the shoes he was wearing with me. Now for the other test."

The other test was still more simple. Every now and then, plainly defined, was a small square hole showing in the soft soil, about three-eighths of an inch in diameter. The detective stuck the walking-stick he was carrying into the ground beside one of these holes. It bore one of those tapering, square ferrules which are common in Alpine walking-sticks. When he removed it from the soil, the impression was exactly the same as the other.

A less shrewd man than Colson would have been perfectly satisfied with the result, and would have made the very natural deduction that Templeton had carried the walking-stick. Indeed, there was every reason to deduce this. But Colson was not only a quick-witted man—he was also a slow and careful thinker. It was his method, when he had discovered any clue, to work out every possible explanation from it mentally raising objections to each deduction. More than once this habit of his had prevented him acting on hasty and erroneous conclusions, and he knew the value of it well.

Besides, this was the biggest case in which he had been engaged. Never yet had he been called upon to investigate so serious a crime as murder, except in one instance, where everything had been fairly obvious from the first. So, for his own credit and chances of promotion, he was anxious to make no mistake.

Therefore, having turned the matter over in his mind, when he reached Frattenbury, instead of going straight to the police station to make his report, he called on Canon Fittleworth. This was in the afternoon, and, it will be remembered, before the Canon had compared the cigar band with those in his box.

"I'm sorry to disturb you," he said, "but you may be able to tell me something. When Mr. Templeton left your house last night, who showed him out?"

"I did," replied the Canon.

"Good. Now can you remember if he was carrying a walking-stick when he left?"

They were standing in the hall as they were talking.

"I can tell you exactly," said the Canon. "He had a stick when he came here—this is it," and he drew one from the rack, "but when we opened the door last night it was clouding up and looked like rain, and the glass was falling. Templeton said he didn't want to risk getting wet, as he suffered from rheumatism. I lent him an umbrella. By the way, I saw it in the cabin of the yacht, now I come to think of it."

Colson had taken the stick into his hand and was examining the point of it. He lifted his eyebrows and gave a low whistle. The ferrule was of the Alpine pattern. He carefully compared it with the one he had brought from Marsh Quay. The sizes were exactly the same.

"What is it?" asked Canon Fittleworth.

"Only a curious coincidence, that throws me entirely out of my reckoning. I'll take this stick, please. Oh, by the way, I went through all the papers I could find on the *Firefly*. There was nothing particular. Only, perhaps you can throw some light on this one."

He took a letter from his pocket and handed it to the Canon. It bore an address in North-West London, and the writer merely said he was glad to hear that Templeton had arrived in England, and hoped that, when he was tired of yachting, he would run up to see him, as there were two or three matters of business to discuss. It was signed "A. F. Crosby."

"Do you know who it is?"

"Why, yes," said the Canon. "I ought to have thought of it before, but this terrible event has put things out of my mind. Templeton mentioned his name last night. He said he was going up to town shortly to see his lawyer, Anthony Crosby. I know him slightly myself. I ought to have written to him. I'll do so at once."

"Oh, that's capital," said Colson. "Don't you trouble to write. We'll 'phone up to the London police, and ask them to see him at once. We must have him down to the inquest to-morrow, if possible. He may be a great help. Thank you very much. I must be off."

When he arrived at the police station he found the superintendent in consultation with the Chief Constable, Major Renshaw, a typical military man with close-cropped moustache.

The two men welcomed the detective-sergeant eagerly.

"Well," said the superintendent, "we're very anxious to know developments. Have you had any luck?"

"Yes, sir—several things have come to light, and there may be something to go upon, though I'm still very much in the dark. First of all, though, I'll get you to have this description 'phoned to the police throughout the county—a young man, a cyclist, staying at the 'Mariner's Arms,' who left suddenly early this morning. The landlady says he was apparently riding into Frattenbury. We ought to get hold of him in any case."

"Most decidedly," said the Chief Constable. "It's important."

After this was done, and the matter of Mr. Crosby taken in hand, the superintendent told Colson that he had telephoned to London about Moss, but, as yet, there were no developments. Then the detective opened his dispatch-case and spread an assortment of articles on the table.

"I made a pretty searching examination," he said, "but I'm afraid there are not many results so far. The lockers and portmanteau mostly contained clothes—and some money. There's only one letter—and there weren't many—that seemed to bear on the case, and it isn't signed. Here it is, in an envelope with the Frattenbury postmark, posted to the G.P.O., Ryde. And it's typewritten."

The letter proved to be a half-sheet of nondescript notepaper, with the words:

"I shall be at home to discuss matters if you will call next Saturday evening after 8.30—not later than 9."

That was all. A grim smile lit up the face of the Chief Constable as he read it, shaking his head.

"That's not much help," he said. "Of course it's the appointment Canon Fittleworth spoke of. What next?"

The detective produced a blotting-pad.

"There's not much here," he said, "but if you hold it before a looking-glass you can make out what I think to be bits of two letters."

Across the top of the blotter, by holding it in front of the glass portions of words appeared as follows:

e y u on turd ft on,

and then the signature, freshly blotted and quite plain:

- *Y rs f ithfully,*
- *R. Templeton.*

" 'See you on Saturday afternoon,' " said the superintendent. "That ought to be plain enough. It looks like his appointment with Moss. We know he went there."

"That's it," said the detective. "Now try the other. That's a puzzler."

For some time the two men scrutinised the blotting-paper. The ink marks were faint and broken, and in most cases only isolated letters, or bits of words. Finally, they agreed with Colson that the result was this:

a d ver zr ice s o ion & roo
s is nal

"Well," said the Chief Constable, "you'll be a smart fellow if you make anything out of *that*—even if it's worth anything. What next?"

"I went through his pockets. There were no papers of any kind in them. That looks suspicious. A gentleman in his position would hardly go about without a pocket-book or something. There was loose cash in the trousers pockets—and in the waistcoat pocket I found this."

He produced a very small bag of chamois leather, with a loose string tied to it to fasten it.

"Look!" he said, as he shook something out on the table.

The two men started. A brilliant coruscation of light flashed before them. It was a diamond the size of a pea.

"Uncut," said the Major, as he took it up to examine it; "in the rough at present, but still brilliant. It's worth a heap of money. And he came from South Africa? Where are the rest?"

"Ah," said the superintendent, "and where does Moss come in?"

"There's something else," said Colson, "and I'm not sure whether it may not be the best clue of all—if we can find the owner of it."

And he laid the two walking-sticks on the table.

"This one," he went on, taking up the one the Canon had given him, "was carried by Templeton when he walked into Frattenbury yesterday afternoon. I've traced the marks of it along the field path. But he didn't take it back with him—Canon Fittleworth lent him an umbrella. And this one," he added, taking up the other, "I found under the stern seat of the dinghy. I'd almost made up my mind it had belonged to Templeton, but inquiry from the Canon seems to show it didn't. After I'd found it I questioned Templeton's man—Webb—though I took care not to let him see it."

"Why not?" asked the Chief Constable.

"Because, sir, I never like to give anything away if I can possibly help it; and I thought, even then, that it might possibly have belonged to someone else. What I wanted to find out from Webb was whether there had been more than one walking-stick aboard the *Firefly*. And there hadn't. So now we know that this stick must have been left by someone else who went out to the yacht."

"Exactly," said the superintendent. "And somebody else knows it, too."

"Who?" asked Major Renshaw.

The superintendent and Colson exchanged meaning glances, and answered simultaneously:

"The man who left it there."

And Colson added:

"He made a bad mistake. And it's mistakes that are the best clues. That's my experience."

The Chief Constable and the superintendent examined the stick carefully. It was a very ordinary plain ash walking-stick, with a crook handle. The only noticeable thing about it was that a small piece had been chipped off the handle. Otherwise there was nothing remarkable about it.

Colson sat lost in thought. Presently his face cleared a little.

"I've got an idea," he said; "it's only a sort of forlorn hope. But I may as well try it. By the way, I promised Gadsden he should be relieved, sir," he added to the superintendent. "He's been at Marsh Quay since early morning."

The superintendent touched a bell, and a constable entered.

"Is Peters in?"

"Yes, sir."

"Tell him to report for duty."

"Very good, sir."

Peters came in, and the superintendent gave him some brief instructions. Then Colson spoke.

"I want you to do exactly what I say, Peters," he said. "When you get to Marsh Quay it will still be daylight. Ride your bicycle there and leave it close to the shore. Then take one of the little canoes and paddle out to the yacht—the *Firefly*. Don't in any way touch the dinghy that's moored to her. Get on the yacht's deck and stay there. Do you understand?"

"Yes, sergeant."

"As soon as it's struck ten—or thereabouts—keep your eye fixed on the upper window in the 'Mariner's Arms.' There may be a light in the room. Don't take any notice of that. But directly you see the flash of a red light in the window, get into the canoe and paddle ashore. Make a bit of noise about it. Leave the canoe in the water—the tide will be flowing—and make the painter fast to one of the posts you will find—well up the little bank. Then light your bicycle lamp and ride off—back to Frattenbury. I shan't want you any more. If there's anybody about, sing out 'Good night' to them—let 'em see you're going off. You understand?"

"I'll do it, sergeant."

"That's all, then. Good night, Major, if I don't see you again. I'll drop in," he added to the superintendent, "before I go back to Marsh Quay. I've got a little job first. And I want this walking-stick."

He went out, carrying the stick he had found in the dinghy.

CHAPTER VI.
Colson is Baffled

Colson walked away from the police station till he came to a shop. It was Sunday and, of course, the shutters were up, but he rang the bell at the side door. It was opened by the proprietor, a thin, sandy-haired man, who shook hands with the detective.

"Good afternoon, Mr. Colson," he said, "come in, won't you? We were just sitting down to tea. The wife will be pleased, I'm sure, if you'll join us."

"No, thank you, Mr. Blake. I'm sorry to disturb you. But I want you to do something for me—if you will?"

Blake looked at him with interest.

"Anything about this murder at Marsh Quay?" he asked. "I heard you were down there."

"Now, look here, Mr. Blake, you and I know one another pretty well. Don't you ask me any questions about that, please. I believe you're a discreet man, or I shouldn't have come to you. Will you hold your tongue about it? About what I'm going to ask you?"

"Of course I will, Mr. Colson."

"Very well. I want you to sell me a walking-stick—on a Sunday. Can we go into your shop?"

"Certainly. Come along."

He led the way into the shop, and turned on the electric light. Whereat it was obvious that Mr. Blake dealt in tobacco, and those other articles which generally characterise a tobacconist's trade.

"What sort of a stick do you want?"

"One exactly like this—if you've got one."

Blake took the stick in his hand and examined it carefully.

"You don't know that stick, I suppose? You haven't seen it before?" asked Colson.

"Can't say I have. It's ordinary enough, eh? With a Swiss ferrule, too. Might have been bought in Switzerland, and might not. We keep a few of these ferrules now—some of our customers prefer them. Let's see—it ought to be easy to find one like it."

A bundle of sticks was laid on the counter. Presently one was found very closely resembling that brought by Colson.

"All right," he said, "this will do—if you can put another ferrule on it."

"That's easily done. Let's be sure it's the exact length—ah—we must take half an inch off it. If you're going to palm it off on anyone as the original, it's a hint to remember that nothing would give it away so much as a difference, however small, in length. Half a minute. My tools are at the back of the shop."

When he returned with the two sticks he said:

"You've noticed yours is chipped a bit in the handle?"

"I know. I'll make the other all right."

"Rub some dirt in when you've done, with a touch of oil. But, there, I expect you know your own job, Mr. Colson. Won't you stay and have tea?"

"I'm busy, thanks."

Colson's next rendezvous was his own home, a pleasant little house a few minutes' walk outside the city walls. And the pleasant little house contained a pleasant little wife, who bustled about to get tea.

"I was wondering if you'd be home to-day, Bob," she said.

"I shall have to be away to-night, my dear. This is going to be a big case, I think."

"Any progress?"

He nodded.

"A little," he said; "tell you all about it when I've finished tea."

No one else knew it, but Colson always took his wife into his confidence. He knew the value of a woman's intuition. And many a time she had helped him at his work with her quick wit.

So, seated by the fire, carefully cutting the stick he had just bought with his knife, he told her all that had happened.

"Have you any idea who did it, Bob?"

"Not the slightest. But there are one or two strong suspicions, eh?"

She nodded.

"You think robbery was the motive?"

"Looks like it—if that little bag had more diamonds in it."

"But why should the thief not take the bag itself—and why should he put it back in Mr. Templeton's waistcoat pocket?"

"Ask me another," he replied.

"Well, here's another, then, Bob. Suppose we grant that the murderer carried this stick. Why was it in the dinghy. You yourself say he must have taken another boat to get to the yacht, because the dinghy was fast to her. How came that stick in the dinghy then?"

"I know," he said slowly. "And it's puzzled me, too."

"Unless——"

"Unless what?"

"Unless Mr. Templeton took someone on board first, someone who laid his walking-stick in the boat while Mr. Templeton rowed him out, and left it there when he was brought back to shore."

Colson brought his hand down on his knee with a smack.

"Good!" he ejaculated. "There may be something in that. It might not belong to the murderer at all. But I'll test it, all the same."

"By the way," went on his wife, "which side of the path were the prints of the stick?"

The detective looked at her with admiration.

"You see that, do you? Well done! They were on the right-hand side as I walked into Frattenbury. That's what made me think—what I've proved from Canon Fittleworth—that Templeton carried it. A man generally carries his stick in his right hand."

She smiled a little as she gazed into the fire, pleased with the compliment.

He had finished cutting the stick now, and was comparing it with the original. Then he rubbed in some dirt and oil. The two sticks looked exactly alike.

"Let me see," said his wife.

She handled them lightly.

"There's a tiny knob just here," and she showed him it on the new stick.

"Bravo! One to you. I'll have that off."

With the most careful scrutiny they both compared the two sticks. The work was completed. Colson rose to go.

"Now, dear," he said, "put some things for the night into my bag and strap it on my bike, please. I'll be back presently. Also, strap on this stick."

"I'll wrap it up in brown paper first," she said. "You can't be too careful."

He kissed her, and went to the police station. Nothing fresh had transpired. He left the stick he had found on the dinghy at the station, wrote out his report, talked over matters with the superintendent, and finally went home to get his bicycle.

Colson was an exceedingly careful man, and instead of taking the Marsh Quay road at once, he started out of the city in the opposite direction and rode by a circuitous route till he reached the southern road by a by-way. When he came to the turning that led to Marsh Quay, he put out his lamp and rode carefully through the darkness, congratulating himself when he reached the "Mariner's Arms" that he had not passed a single person.

Mrs. Yates had provided a tempting supper of cold meat, pickles, cheese and beer, and while the detective was doing full justice to it, came into his room.

"They've all gone now, sir," she said; "there's no one else in the house."

"That's all right. Well, I suppose they talked about the murder, eh?"

"Nothing else, Mr. Colson. A lot o' rubbish they talked, too. There's nothing I overheard 'em say that's worth mentioning."

"I see. Well, now, look here, Mrs. Yates. I want you to leave the front door on the latch, and if you hear me go downstairs in the night, don't you take any notice, see?"

"Very good, sir. Anything more you want?"

"No, thank you, Mrs. Yates; you can clear away. Only, don't take my glass. I haven't finished your excellent beer yet."

When she had bid him good night, he lighted his pipe and leaned back in his chair, thinking over the events of the day, sipping his beer from time to time. Presently he looked at his watch. It was a little after ten. Taking a small piece of red glass from his pocket, he lifted the lamp from the table and approached the window with it. He held the bit of glass in front of the lamp for a few minutes and then put out the light.

He opened the window. It was a cloudy night and very dark. He could hear Gadsden paddling himself ashore, and could just discern a dim form as he landed. Gadsden was making plenty of noise. He lighted his bicycle lamp, mounted his machine, and rode off, sounding his bell as he did so. Colson heard him shout out "Good night" when he was a little way down the road.

He sat by the window for some little time. Then, first putting on a pair of rubber-soled tennis shoes, and taking with him the stick he had brought from Frattenbury, first unwrapping it from its brown paper covering, he slipped quietly downstairs and went out.

Very carefully picking his way, he went down to the shore. It was a perfectly quiet night, the silence only broken by the ripple of the tide flowing up the estuary. He looked around him. Only one light was burning—in a window of Mr. Proctor's house. The latter had evidently not yet gone to bed.

Colson unhitched the painter from the post, slowly, without making a sound, launched the canoe, and paddled out in silence. Arrived beside the dinghy, he placed the walking-stick well under the seat, where he had found the original, and returned just as quietly to the shore.

Before he went back to the inn he took careful stock of another canoe that was close to the shore, and gave a nod of satisfaction. Then he returned to his room and waited and watched.

As he had said, it was a forlorn hope and he hardly expected that anything would come of it. It was more than probable that the murderer was miles away by this time. And yet, if that stick *had* belonged to him, so far as Colson knew at present, it was the only clue to the mystery. And whoever had left it in the dinghy must know that as well. The point that Colson was building upon was the fact that the stick had been stowed away under the seat of the dinghy and was not found on board the yacht itself. If it belonged to the man who had committed the crime, there was just the chance that he might calculate that little notice had been taken of the dinghy. And it would be worth something to him to get it back.

It was some time after midnight that Colson gave a start and stood tense at the window. A slight sound had disturbed him. Straining his eyes through the darkness, he could just discern a form apparently bending over one of the canoes on the shore. Then he saw the form straighten itself and walk a little distance away. He lost sight of it, but in a few moments it returned. Again it bent down.

"He's unfastening the painter," murmured the detective. Then he could see a man get into the canoe, and the next moment he could hear the slight splash of a paddle. The unknown was making for the yacht.

Colson felt the little automatic pistol he carried in his pocket—he was taking no risks. Quickly he made his way downstairs, opened the door and went out, crouching low. It was his intention to get down to the shore, lie hidden behind one of the boats, and catch the unknown unawares as he landed. He looked across the water. The canoe was alongside the dinghy now. He had to act quickly to get to his hiding-place.

Then the unlucky thing happened. He caught his foot in a low post, and went sprawling on the stones with a crash that rang out in the still night. Colson swore roundly beneath his breath, picked himself up, and rushed to the water's edge. He knew he was discovered. Then, to his dismay, he heard the splash of the paddle and could just see the canoe shooting out beyond the yacht into the estuary.

He rushed for one of the other canoes, whipped out his knife, cut the painter, and pushed her into the water. But as he stepped in he swore again.

"Confound my luck," he muttered; "there's no paddle. *That's what he was up to.*"

Looking out over the estuary, he saw the dim form of the canoe and its occupant rapidly shooting up with the tide towards Frattenbury. By the time he had found the paddle—thrown on the grass thirty yards away or so—it was too late. The tide was running like a mill-stream.

Again cursing his bad luck, he paused for a minute to reflect. What could he do? Nothing. The man might land on either bank, or at the extremity of the estuary—anywhere. For a moment he thought of mounting his bicycle, but the only road it was possible to ride was round by Frattenbury. To attempt to follow up by running along the side of the estuary in such a dark night would be equally fruitless for fast going. The canoe would be running up that tide race with great speed, and the occupant had every chance of escaping. Marsh Quay had neither telephone nor telegraph; it was impossible to head him off by sending a message to the Frattenbury police.

Colson shook his fist at the estuary, a disappointed man. To make quite sure that the unknown had come for the walking-stick he paddled out to the dinghy. It was a foregone conclusion. There was no stick there.

He returned to the inn. There was nothing more to be done.

"There's one thing, though," he said as he undressed; "I've got the original stick still, *and he doesn't know it.* That's a point to me, and it may mean that I'll have him yet."

Colson was one of those fortunate individuals who can do with very little sleep. He woke at an early hour, fresh and alert.

He glanced out of the window as he was dressing.

The tide was on the ebb. A canoe was out in mid-stream, a man in her paddling down from the upper reach. As he drew nearer and began to turn towards the shore, the detective recognised him. It was Mr. Proctor.

Hastily Colson slipped on the rest of his clothes, and was on the shore just as Mr. Proctor came in. The detective pursed up his lips as he recognised the canoe. It was the one in which the unknown had made his escape in the night.

Proctor was the first to speak as he stepped ashore. He smiled and nodded affably.

"Good morning," he said. "You're an early bird, Mr. Colson."

"So are you," retorted the detective dryly. "Been out fishing?"

"No," said the little man. "I've been rescuing my canoe. Some joker seems to have played tricks with it in the night."

"What do you mean?" asked the detective, looking at him intently.

But the little man returned his gaze quite calmly.

"Why," he said, "my energetic young nephew went out eel-spearing at some unearthly hour—to catch the falling tide—walks on the mud, you know, with what we call cleat boards fixed to his boots. It's a good place for eels further up the estuary. About half a mile up he came on my canoe, stranded on a ridge of stones. He couldn't get her down to the water by himself, so he ran home and woke me. Now, I should like to know who took that canoe out last night."

The detective thought he would like to know also.

"I suppose it wasn't you—or any of your police people, eh?" went on the little man. "I know in a case like this you're up to all kinds of funny little dodges."

"No," replied Colson, "it wasn't any of us. Our man—Constable Gadsden—came back to Frattenbury quite early last night. There was nothing to keep him here."

He looked hard again at Mr. Proctor as he spoke. He was getting a little puzzled. But the other man was apparently quite calm.

"Well," he said, "I'm going to get some breakfast. I suppose you had yours before you came out from Frattenbury this morning?"

It was an innocent enough question, but Colson was on his guard.

"As a matter of fact, I didn't," he said. "I'm going to see if I can get some at the 'Mariner's Arms.'"

Proctor nodded and turned to go.

"One moment," said the detective. "I should like to see your nephew about finding that canoe this morning."

"What?" retorted Proctor, stopping and turning. "Do you think there's anything in it about the murder?"

"I never said that. But it's best to take notice of anything, you know."

"Very well, then, come in after breakfast and see him."

The detective ate his meal in silence. There were several matters which gave him food for his mind as well as for his body. He was getting profoundly dissatisfied with the course of events. When Mrs. Yates came into the room to clear away he asked her, casually, how long Mr. Proctor had been living at Marsh Quay.

"About two years, sir. The house was for sale then, and he came and bought it. A nice gentleman he is, too."

"Does he do anything?"

"Just a bit of boatin' and fishin', that's all. He ain't got cause to work for his living. They say he's retired from his business, whatever it was I dunno."

"Married?"

"No, sir. He's a bachelor. Would you like a bit o' fish for your dinner, Mr. Colson? I can get some nice fresh whiting."

"Excellent, Mrs. Yates. Keep your mouth shut about my sleeping here last night. If anyone's inquisitive, make 'em think I came out from Frattenbury early this morning."

"I will, sir."

He strolled across to Mr. Proctor's house. The latter saw him coming through the window, and opened the door for him.

"Can I offer you a smoke?" he said. "A cigarette—or——"

"Thanks, I stick to my pipe. You don't mind my lighting up?"

"Go on—have some of this," and he set a tobacco jar on the table. "Now, Phil," he went on to the boy who was with him "you must tell the detective-sergeant how you found my canoe this morning."

Colson listened while the boy told his story, which was brief and simple. And as he listened his gaze strayed once or twice to a picture, a large framed photograph, hanging over the mantelpiece. He asked Philip a few questions.

"Was she fastened in any way?"

"No—just lying on the stones."

"Just as she might have been left if anyone had landed from her when the tide was up, eh?"

"Yes."

"I see. I expect you know all about the tide here, don't you?"

"Rather," said the boy.

"Then what time do you calculate the tide was up to the spot where you found her?"

"That's no use," said Philip promptly. "You see, if the fellow landed before high tide the flow would go on washing the canoe up and leave her stranded when it turned. I found her at highwater mark, of course."

The detective, who had his eyes riveted on Proctor's face while the boy was replying, smiled approvingly.

"You're a sharp lad," he said. "I ought to have thought of that. But it means that he landed either at or before high tide, eh?"

"That's it," said the boy.

Colson got up to go, lingering a little in the room. He strolled up to the fire-place casually.

"That's a fine view," he said, nodding towards the picture. "Looks like a bit of Switzerland."

"It is," replied Proctor. "It's the Julier Pass, just before you get into the Engadine."

"Ah! I've always wanted to spend a holiday in Switzerland, but I've never been able to run to it. You've been there, I suppose?" he asked Proctor, turning to him as he spoke.

"Oh, yes—some years ago."

"I see. Well, thank you very much, sir. I won't hinder you any longer."

"I shall see you this afternoon," said the little man, in the act of showing him out. "I'm summoned on the jury."

Philip had come to the door with them. The detective turned to him.

"Did you get good sport with the eels this morning?" he asked.

"Not so bad. It's ripping sport. Have you tried it?"

"No," laughed the detective. "What sort of a spear do you use?"

"Come along. I'll show you. I left it in the garden here."

Colson followed him, examined the spear, chatting as he did so.

"And you say about half a mile up yonder—near the spot where you found the canoe—is the best place for eels?"

"Yes. I always go there."

"I see. Well, if you get up so early you may make your uncle think there's a burglar in the house—if he hears you about in the dark, you know, eh?"

"It wasn't dark when I got up," said the boy, a little surprised, "and uncle knew I was going out this morning early. I told him so last night."

"Can't quite make out that uncle of yours," said Colson to himself as he walked along. "I wonder if he is only a fool."

CHAPTER VII.
The Inquest

The coroner arrived a little early, and was standing on the shore with the Chief Constable and the superintendent, the latter pointing out to him the scene of the crime.

"Shocking, shocking!" he exclaimed in his dry, formal manner. "I have your detailed report, Mr. Superintendent. I suppose there's nothing else I ought to know before we begin?"

"I don't think so."

"Well, I hope we shall catch the scoundrel," remarked the Chief Constable, giving a twist to his moustache, as they turned away towards the inn. "He deserves hanging if ever a man did."

"Precisely. He does, indeed," replied the coroner. "That, of course, is *your* business. Mine is only to ascertain the circumstances and the cause of death." He took out his watch. "It's about time we began," he went on.

When the jury filed into the bar parlour after viewing the body they found none too much space. The room barely accommodated them, the police, the witnesses, and representatives of the Press. Outside the inn a little crowd of people had to be content with waiting patiently.

The coroner took his seat at the top of the table, near the fireplace, which was in an angle of the room. Seated on his right, facing across the table, and therefore at the other angle, was Mr. Proctor, who had been elected by the jury as their foreman. Facing the coroner sat the police and the doctor. On one side of the room was a tall man with clean-shaven face and a professional manner. He was Mr. Anthony Crosby, the lawyer from London.

The coroner opened the proceedings formally by explaining to the jury their duties, concluding by saying:

"It will probably be necessary to adjourn this inquiry, and in that case you will not be called upon to record your verdict this afternoon. I think, from what I have said, you will quite understand that the scope of this inquiry is limited to the actual cause of death and circumstances which may throw light upon such cause. Of course, if anything transpires which may assist the police in their investigations, I shall exercise my prerogative in allowing it to be brought forward. But the jury are not concerned with police investigations other than those which threw light upon the actual cause of death. I hope I make myself plain?"

And he turned an inquiring look upon Mr. Proctor.

The little man nodded his bald head.

"I think I can say on behalf of the jury, sir, that we all understand perfectly."

"Very well," said the coroner. "Now we can proceed with the inquiry."

Whereupon Anthony Crosby rose from his seat and said:

"I represent the late Mr. Templeton, sir—as his legal adviser."

"Your name?" asked the coroner.

"Mr. Anthony Crosby, of Crosby and Paxton, 17B, Lincoln's Inn Fields."

The coroner bowed and made a note of it.

The first witness called was Jim Webb, who gave evidence of the discovery of the body early on the previous morning. The coroner asked him a few questions.

"You say that the deceased had arranged to go into Frattenbury on the Saturday afternoon?"

"Yes, sir."

"And that you were given the night off?"

"Yes, sir."

"Tell me, did you know whom he was going to see?"

"The Reverend Fittleworth, sir. I guessed it afterwards."

The coroner elevated his eyebrows.

"*Guessed* it? What do you mean? How did you guess it?"

The man explained that he had read Canon Fittleworth's name and address on the letter he had posted for his master.

"Were you in the habit of prying into Mr. Templeton's correspondence?" asked the coroner sarcastically.

Jim Webb reddened.

"No, sir, I wasn't," he replied emphatically.

"Oh! How many more names and addresses did you read?"

"Not any, sir. As a matter of fact that was the only letter he ever gave me to post."

"You're sure? Remember you are on oath."

"Quite sure, sir."

"Very well."

Anthony Crosby interposed just as Webb was about to stand down.

"May I put a question to the witness?"

"Yes—if you wish. It should be done through me."

"Thank you, sir. Will you ask him if he can give an account of his actions from Saturday evening till Sunday morning?"

"You hear the question," said the coroner to Webb; "what have you to say?"

"Of course I can," said the man, a little indignantly. "I was in my uncle's house at Frattenbury. I can bring three witnesses to prove that."

"Are you satisfied?" the coroner asked Crosby.

"Perfectly, thank you."

"You ought to be grateful for that question," said the coroner to Webb, who was muttering something; "it clears you in the eyes of the jury of any connection with the crime. Next witness, please."

The next witness was the doctor, who gave his evidence tersely and technically. Several times the coroner had to ask him to explain surgical terms to the jury.

"How long do you consider he had been dead?" asked the coroner.

"Some hours—I would not undertake to say precisely how many."

"Well—before or after midnight?"

"Probably before. Possibly after."

"You will not commit yourself?"

"No."

"You think he was stabbed with a knife?"

"I do not. I consider that the weapon was more in the form of a dagger. The wound was distinctly triangular."

"And that death was instantaneous?"

"Death was instantaneous."

"There were no signs of a struggle?"

"None. I am of opinion that the deceased was probably seated on the bunk, leaning towards the table, that he fell forward, struck his head against the table, and then pitched onto the floor of the cabin. There was a slight abrasion on the left temple which makes this probable."

After one or two further questions the doctor resumed his seat. He was followed by Tom Gale, who gave evidence as to the arrival of the yacht and the crossing of the estuary by the murdered man. When he had finished, the coroner addressed the superintendent.

"You have this matter in hand?" he asked.

"We have, sir. I should like to suggest that it is strictly a question for the police at this moment."

"Certainly," replied the coroner. "The jury will please note it. It may have a bearing on the case at a further stage of the inquiry. I think that is what you mean?"

"Quite so, sir," replied the superintendent. "Thank you."

The superintendent himself was next called upon. Briefly and clearly he described his visit to the yacht the previous morning, corroborating the non-technical portion of the doctor's evidence. The coroner leaned back in his chair, the tips of his fingers together, and thought for a moment. Then he said:

"A thorough investigation of the cabin was made, I presume?"

"Yes, sir. I placed it in the hands of Detective-Sergeant Colson."

"Is there any matter in connection with that investigation which you consider the jury ought to know?"

"At present, sir, I would rather not advance any information—except to say that there is nothing which would assist the jury in arriving at their verdict. And I ask for an adjournment of the inquiry when all the witnesses called to-day have been heard."

The coroner nodded.

"That is quite reasonable," he said, "quite reasonable."

Mr. Crosby rose.

"In my position," he said, "I should naturally wish further questions to be put to the witness, but I shall be perfectly satisfied if I have an assurance from the police that they will give me any information which may be of use to me."

"You will do this?" asked the coroner.

"Most certainly," replied the superintendent. "Our wish is only that certain details may not become public."

The next witness was Canon Fittleworth. He had known the coroner for years, fairly intimately, and he smiled a little as that functionary asked his name, address and occupation as though he were an entire stranger. He told the jury the facts he had already put before the superintendent. Rather a lengthy examination followed, in the course of which the coroner asked him:

"You say the deceased informed you he had business with someone in Frattenbury on Saturday night?"

"He did."

"You do not know with whom?"

"No."

"He did not tell you?"

"He did not."

"He did not drop any hint?"

"No."

"You knew Mr. Templeton fairly intimately—didn't he mention anyone he knew in Frattenbury? It is an important point."

"I did not know him very intimately. I hadn't seen him for some years. So far as I am aware, he knew no one in Frattenbury except myself and family."

"You have no idea what this business was that he mentioned?"

"Not exactly."

"What do you mean by 'not exactly'?"

The coroner was looking at the Canon keenly. The jury were interested.

"Only that, in the course of conversation, he mentioned that he was glad to be getting rid of something valuable he had been carrying about for a long time."

"What was it?"

"He didn't say."

"You are sure?"

"Yes."

"Thank you, Canon Fittleworth. That will do. You will allow me—and I am sure the jury will join me in this—you will allow us to express our very deep sympathy towards you and our family in this terrible tragedy."

The Canon bowed.

"Thank you," he said. "There is—er—a statement I wish to make—something in the way of evidence."

"What is it?" asked the coroner.

"When I went on board the yacht yesterday morning there was something I found in the cabin—something I ought, perhaps, to have given to the police—but my mind was so much agitated at the time."

The superintendent and Colson looked up quickly. The coroner asked sharply:

"What was it?"

"A band off a cigar—lying on the floor of the cabin—here it is," and he laid it on the table.

The jury leaned forward—it was a moment of intense interest—the coroner motioned for the cigar band to be passed to him, took and examined it. Then he sat still thinking, leaning back in his chair, his head bent down. Then he said:

"You think this important?"

"I do."

"Why?"

"Because my cousin did not smoke. He told me so on Saturday evening."

The coroner sat bolt upright in his chair, a frown on his face, his eyes literally glaring at the Canon.

"The jury must see this. Pass it round," he exclaimed.

Then he went on with great severity:

"You must forgive my saying, Canon Fittleworth, that I consider you have behaved in an exceedingly careless manner. I have no doubt that you did not think—as you say—but a man of your intelligence ought to have thought. This should have been handed to the police immediately. It is just such want of thought that often leads to grave hindrances of justice. I am sorry to have to say this, but, in my position here, it is only my duty."

He had leaned forward as he spoke, his elbows on the table. As he resumed his former upright position, his right elbow swept one or two papers off the table. They fell fluttering into the fire-place. He leaned over to the right to pick them up, but before he could do so the foreman of the jury went down on one knee to assist him.

The coroner picked up one bit of paper, Proctor the rest.

"Thanks," said the coroner as the foreman handed them to him.

Meanwhile, the cigar band was being passed from man to man of the jury. Each of them examined it solemnly and portentously, one or two shaking their heads with an air of profound wisdom. So it went round till it reached the foreman, and his examination was the longest of all. He pursed up his little round mouth, adjusted a pair of spectacles on his nose, and looked carefully at the little red and gold object. Finally, as though loath to part with it, he handed it to two of the jurymen across the table who had not yet seen it, and they passed it on to the coroner.

Meanwhile, the Canon was standing with burning face. It was a new and humiliating experience for a cathedral dignitary to be soundly rated in public, and though, in his heart of hearts, he admitted the justice of it, he was exceedingly irritated.

"I much regret," he said stiffly, and a little pompously—"I much regret what you are pleased to call my indiscretion, but I am not accustomed to experiences of this nature. I can say no more."

"Have you anything to add?" asked the coroner, relenting a little, but still stern.

If the worthy Canon had been feeling normal he might have said more. But he was so acutely concerned with what he considered an undignified situation that he merely remarked:

"Nothing. Except that the brand is that of a particular cigar which I smoke myself."

It was here that the foreman of the jury interposed:

"May I ask a question?"

But the coroner, after a moment's thought, said:

"You may ask me to put a question if you please, but in the interests of the case I imagine the police would rather you did not."

And the Chief Constable, who had been in whispered consultation with the superintendent and Colson, immediately exclaimed:

"Thank you. We much prefer that no questions should be asked. We consider this matter as strictly belonging to the police—at this stage of the inquiry."

"I think it does," replied the coroner. "I shall hand over this cigar band to you, of course."

And he laid it on the table. There was one man who never took his eyes off it for a moment, and that was the detective, who put it in his pocket-case a minute or two later when the inquiry was formally adjourned.

"You may stand down, Canon Fittleworth," said the coroner stiffly. "Are there any more witnesses?"

There were none.

"You ask for an adjournment," said the coroner to the superintendent, "for how long?"

"This day fortnight, sir."

The coroner consulted his diary. "Will Saturday week do?" he asked. "I have a case in court on the Monday."

"That will do very well, sir," replied the superintendent.

The majority pressed out of the tap-room, Colson and Anthony Crosby being among the few who remained. The doctor, who had motored Canon Fittleworth over to Marsh Quay, was in a hurry to get back. As the latter got into the car, the superintendent came up and said, more in sorrow than in anger:

"You ought to have given us that cigar band at once, really you ought, sir."

"I know I ought," said the Canon, whose injured pride was beginning to thaw. "I'm sorry."

"I'll call later on, if I may—or Colson will—we shall want to see your particular brand of cigars."

"Do!"

But when Colson and the superintendent made a closer examination of that cigar band, they agreed that it might not be worth while troubling the worthy Canon.

"These parsons aren't much help," said Colson sarcastically; "they'd best stick to preaching and not mix themselves up in our business. Bother the blighter! I say."

"I say—how did you manage to miss that cigar band, on the yacht?" asked the superintendent.

"I can tell you exactly, sir. I made my examination while the body was on the floor. When they came to lay it out on the table I went on deck—I was still there when you and the Canon came aboard, you remember? I made a further examination afterwards, but that band must have been under Templeton's body in the first place. That would account for the Canon finding it."

CHAPTER VIII.
Winnie Cotterill Pays a Visit to Frattenbury

"Hurry up, Winnie, breakfast is all ready."

"All right," came a voice from somewhere, "I'll be with you in a minute. You begin—don't wait for me."

Maude Wingrave seated herself at the breakfast table and poured out a cup of tea. It was a tiny room, high up in a block of flats, looking over Battersea Park. The girl who sat at the table was short and dark-haired, with a merry expression on her somewhat plain face.

"You are the limit, Winnie," she exclaimed as a newcomer entered the room, a girl of about five and twenty, with a fresh, clear-cut face and grey eyes. "You're a downright lazy pig."

"I can't help it. I simply *hate* getting up. What's for breakfast? I'm hungry."

"Go on—help yourself. Do something towards running this establishment, if it's only *that*. I've not too much time. Can't look after you."

And she glanced at her wrist-watch.

"You ought to be thankful, Winnie Cotterill, that you don't have to keep office hours."

"I am," replied Winnie. "Providence never intended me to be punctual, so Providence has provided me with work that doesn't need a 9 a.m. beginning each day. Pass the toast."

"What are you doing to-day?"

"Finishing the cover of the Christmas number of *Peter's Magazine*, my dear, and I'm thankful to get it off my hands. Then I'm going seriously to tackle that short story the editor of *The Holborn* sent me to illustrate. A 'horrible murder,' Maude. With a detective in it. I'm going to make him a little ugly, snubbed-nose creature, wearing big police boots. True to life, my dear—none of your impossible Sherlock Holmes."

The other girl laughed.

"I've got an interview with our new 'serial' this morning," she said—"a great big man of fifty, with a solemn beard and spectacles. He's selling us the most romantic piffle you ever read. There'll be a boom in our issue when the servant girls get hold of it. Hand over the paper if you're not using it. I want to glance at the news before I go."

Winnie Cotterill passed the newspaper to her friend. Maude Wingrave opened it.

"Hallo!" she exclaimed, "talk about your story with a 'horrible murder' in it—here's a real one!"

"What is it?"

Maude read out the head-lines:

"*Mysterious Crime.*"

"*Yachtsman Murdered on Board His Yacht.*"

"*Inquest To-day.*"

"Who is it?" asked Winnie, as she reached over for the teapot.

Maude began to read:

"*Early yesterday morning a shocking discovery was made on board a small yacht, anchored in the little harbour of Marsh Quay, on an estuary of the Channel, about two miles from the cathedral city of Frattenbury. Mr. Reginald Templeton, a Fellow of the Royal Geographical Society, only lately returned from South Africa——*"

Winnie Cotterill dropped her knife and fork on her plate.

"Who?" she exclaimed.

"Mr. Reginald Templeton. Why?"

"Oh, my dear!"

"What is it?"

"Pass me the paper. It must be—yes—it *is*—murdered! Oh, Maude!"

"Do you know him?"

"Why, of course I do! Ever since I can remember. He was a great friend of my mother, and always so kind to me. I always called him Uncle. Why, I only had a letter from him last week. He was coming to London, soon, he said."

"Oh, you poor dear! Are you *sure* it's the same man, Winnie?"

"It must be," said the girl, looking at the paper again. "Yes—when he wrote he said he was yachting on the South Coast. Oh, Maude, what am I to do?"

Maude had risen from the seat and was looking over her friend's shoulder.

"Look," she said, pointing with her finger, "he'd been dining the night before with his cousin, Canon Fittleworth. Do you know him?"

"I've heard Uncle speak of him. No, I've never met him."

"Why not write to him—or telegraph?"

Winnie shook her head.

"I don't know," she replied. "Of course, you see, Mr. Templeton isn't any relation of mine. But I was awfully fond of him. Poor old Uncle! I know what I *will* do, dear," she went on impulsively.

"What?"

"I *must* finish that cover this morning. But I'll go down to Frattenbury this afternoon and see Canon Fittleworth—yes, I will."

Maude had glanced at her watch again, and was putting on her gloves.

"Will it be any good?" she asked.

"Oh, Maude, I *must*! He's been so awfully good to me. Why, my dear, when my mother died, and there wasn't a penny, it was Mr. Templeton who paid for my art training. I owe my living to him—really. Don't you see?"

Maude nodded her head sympathetically.

"I know, dear. I should do just the same. I'm *so* sorry. Yes—go down to Frattenbury. I wish I could go with you, but I simply *have* to get to the office."

"Don't worry about me, dear. I shall take a handbag in case I stay the night—I can get a room at an hotel. I'll wire and let you know if I'm not coming back this evening."

"Thanks. I'd like to know. Good-bye!"

And she nodded brightly as she left the room to go to her work. She was sub-editress of one of the many popular weeklies issued by a well-known firm of publishers and newspaper proprietors. The two "bachelor" girl friends had been sharing the same flat for nearly a year.

Winnie Cotterill slowly finished her breakfast, reading the details of the tragedy as she did so—a couple of columns in the usual blaring journalistic style, followed by a short article on local police methods, detrimental, of course, to the said local police. She was getting into a calmer frame of mind now, though still much upset by the shock of hearing such unexpected news.

Breakfast over, she went into the little adjacent room she dignified by the name of "studio" and got to work on the magazine cover. When it was finished, she took a bus to Fleet Street and deposited it with her editor, in whose office she consulted a Bradshaw.

She had already packed a small handbag and, after a light lunch at a restaurant, she caught the afternoon train to Frattenbury, arriving about six, and at once made her way to the Close.

Canon Fittleworth was closeted in his study with Anthony Crosby, who had returned from Marsh Quay and was staying the night at an hotel. A maid announced the fact that a young lady wished to see the Canon, and handed him a visiting card on a salver.

The Canon adjusted his pince-nez and read the name out loud.

"Miss Winifred Cotterill."

"Eh?" interjaculated the lawyer, looking up from some papers he was studying.

"Miss Winifred Cotterill," repeated the Canon. "I don't know her."

"But I do," said Anthony Crosby, "at least, I know of her. She is, in a way, connected with this case, and I was going to communicate with her as soon as I got back to London."

"Oh, well, in that case, we'll see her together. Show Miss Cotterill in, Jane."

The Canon looked her over quickly as she entered. He was, for the moment, half afraid that there might have been some unpleasant incident in his cousin's life, with some undesirable female connected with it. His suspicions were quickly removed. He saw a neatly-dressed girl with a refined and pleasant face, and took a step towards her.

"Miss Cotterill?"

"I'm afraid I must apologise. I came down to Frattenbury because—because I read about Mr. Templeton's murder in the paper this morning, and you are his cousin, and——"

"Now do sit down, Miss Cotterill," interrupted the Canon, "and before I ask you anything else—have you had any tea?"

"I've only just arrived," replied the girl.

"I thought so. Now, I'm going to ring for tea. I'm sure you want some, and then you can tell us all about it. Mr. Crosby," and he waved his hand in introduction towards the lawyer, "heard your name when it was announced, and says he knows of you."

Winnie Cotterill looked surprised.

"You know me?" she asked.

"I've heard about you, Miss Cotterill," said the lawyer. "You see, I had the privilege of being a friend of Mr. Templeton, as well as his legal adviser, and he mentioned you several times. I quite understand what a shock this terrible affair must be to you."

"He was most awfully kind to me," said the girl, her voice quavering a little, "and I felt I must come down and find out more about it."

Anthony Crosby nodded sympathetically. The maid brought in tea. Winnie Cotterill explained how Mr. Templeton had been a friend of her mother, and what he had done for her. Then she listened while the Canon told her about the murder.

"But why, *why* was he murdered?" she asked. "I can't understand."

"Ah, my dear young lady," said the Canon, "that is what we all want to know. We suspect that robbery was the cause of it and, of course, the police have it in hand. Now tell me," and he looked at his watch, "I naturally take an interest in any friend of my poor cousin. Were you thinking of going back to London to-night? I ask because the funeral will take place to-morrow afternoon—the coroner has given an order for burial—and I thought you might like to be present."

"I should, very much," replied the girl, "and I'll get a bed at an hotel for to-night. Perhaps you can tell me of one?"

She had risen to go.

"Sit down and have another cup of tea," said the Canon with a smile. "I'll be back in a minute or two."

He came back with his wife. Mrs. Fittleworth greeted the girl warmly.

"You poor thing!" she said; "my husband has just told me about you. I'm so sorry. But you mustn't think of going to an hotel. Do let us put you up for the night."

"It's very kind of you."

"Nonsense. Of course you will stay with us. Come along, you must be very tired."

She took the girl out of the room, and the two men were left together. The Canon looked inquiringly at Anthony Crosby. The latter took a cigarette from his case, tapped it deliberately, lighted it, and began.

"I was going to tell you about Miss Cotterill, anyhow," he said. "From all I have gathered, you know very little of your late cousin?"

"Very little indeed. I so rarely saw him. And he was a reticent man. I really know nothing at all about his affairs."

The lawyer nodded.

"Yes," he agreed, "he was distinctly reticent, I know. I suppose *I* know as much as anyone, and that isn't a great deal. Now, about this girl—I speak in confidence, of course?"

"Of course."

"Well, Templeton—like most men—had a romance in his life."

"He never married."

"No," said the lawyer deliberately, "the other man did that—it was years ago now."

"Who was the woman?" asked the Canon, his curiosity aroused.

"This girl's mother," replied Crosby. "That is as much as he told me. She was left a widow when Winifred was about five years old—as far as I understand."

"Why didn't he marry her then?"

The lawyer smiled grimly.

"I always consider that parsons, doctors and we lawyers have more chances of knowing about human nature than the rest of the world. And you ought to know that very often when a man doesn't get his first chance of marrying the woman he loves, he won't take a second chance when it comes. That's the only answer I can give you."

"Yes—it's often true," said the Canon thoughtfully. "I've seen it more than once."

"Exactly. Well, the fact remains that Templeton didn't marry Mrs. Cotterill. But he stood by her and her child. The girl has told you he paid for her training as an art student."

The Canon nodded.

"Just so. Well, before he went abroad to South Africa he came to me and asked me to draw up his will. I have it at my office. If there isn't a later one, of course, it stands good for probate."

"I see."

Crosby flicked the ash off his cigarette and smiled at the Canon.

"I'm afraid you won't benefit by it," he said.

Canon Fittleworth laughed.

"It's no disappointment," he replied; "I never expected anything."

"Then I hope that, as his nearest relative, as I suppose you are, you won't be envious when I tell you he has left everything he possesses to this girl—Winifred Cotterill."

"Indeed?" said Canon Fittleworth. "No, I'm not a bit envious. The girl is an orphan, and I'm only too glad. Besides, after what you tell me, it's perfectly natural. Romance has a strange sway over human affairs."

"But," said the other slowly and deliberately, "unless Templeton made anything out of his last venture—which I doubt—it won't be very much—not two thousand pounds."

"I see—I knew nothing of his affairs. But I always imagined him to be comfortably off."

"He should have been—but for my profession," said the lawyer. "No, don't blame me. I did the best I could for him, but he would not listen to reason. He got involved, some years ago, in an unfortunate and expensive lawsuit—a question of adjacent properties. I advised him, at the time, to compromise, but he was adamant. The case went against him, and he insisted upon carrying it to the Court of Appeal. The appeal was quashed—as I knew it would be. The costs were enormous—he insisted on having the best counsel—and he had to sell the whole of his property to pay them. The other man bought the property, and Templeton never forgave him."

"I remember hearing something about it at the time," said the Canon. "So that was why he sold the little place in Buckinghamshire! What a pity! I suppose he was in the wrong, though?"

"I didn't say that," replied the other dryly. "It was a case of law. And I admit that the law is not always just. Anyhow, he became a comparatively poor man. Besides, he spent what money he had on travelling. An explorer, out on his own, can't expect to make money unless he discovers a gold-mine. And Templeton didn't. Even if he had, he'd not the business capacity to make anything out of it. Poor chap! 'De mortuis,' eh?"

"Quite so," said the Canon. After a silence he remarked:

"Are you going to tell the girl—now?"

Anthony Crosby shook his head.

"Not for the moment," he replied. "I prefer to act professionally. As a matter of fact, I didn't bring the will. It's at my office, and I had to come straight down here from my home. Besides, there's a sealed packet that Templeton handed me just before he sailed—only to be opened by me in the event of his death. It may contain a codicil, or even another will. So it wouldn't be fair to tell her yet, you see. You won't say anything about it, will you?"

"Of course I won't. Must you be going now?"

For the lawyer had risen.

"I must. I'm staying at the 'Dolphin,' and I've some letters to write. I shall see you to-morrow—at the funeral. I want to have a consultation with the police in the morning."

It was about ten o'clock that evening that the Canon, who had retired to his study after dinner, came into the drawing-room. His wife and daughter and Winnie Cotterill were seated there.

"Who was with you in the study, dear?" asked his wife. "I heard Jane showing someone in."

"Major Renshaw," replied her husband, seating himself. "He came in to have a smoke and discuss the events of the day."

Mrs. Fittleworth glanced swiftly at Winnie Cotterill. With a woman's instinct she knew the girl had had nearly enough strain that day. She was just going to try to turn the conversation when the Canon went on in his best parsonical manner that brooked no interruption:

"Of course, I refrained from asking him very much about any possible clues, and so on," he said. "The police naturally wish to keep these things to themselves. But he did tell me something, which isn't exactly private, because it's being talked about at Marsh Quay. There was a young man lodging at the inn there—the 'Mariner's Arms.' An artist, apparently, though no one seems to know anything about him."

"Go on, father," said Doris; "this sounds most exciting."

"Well, the strange thing is that he left quite suddenly yesterday morning—just before the unhappy affair was discovered. The landlady says he came downstairs very early and announced his intention of leaving at once."

The three women were listening intently. The Canon went on:

"He was, it seems, cycling into Frattenbury. But he never went there. The police have been making inquiries, and only found out this evening that he stayed last night at Selham—three miles from Marsh Quay down the estuary, you know. He left there this morning, so they say, and must have been close to Marsh Quay, because he was seen riding in the direction of Frattenbury. Then all trace of him was lost again."

"Oh, daddy, how exciting! Do they think he committed the murder?"

"Well, Renshaw didn't say that—but, of course, it's suspicious going off like that, and the police are making every effort to find him. They have his description, and it shouldn't be difficult."

"Do they know his name?" asked Mrs. Fittleworth.

"They know the name under which he stayed at the inn," replied the Canon, "but, of course, it may be a fictitious one."

"What is it, daddy?"

"Grayson—Harold Grayson."

"Oh!"

They all turned towards Winnie Cotterill, from whom the exclamation proceeded. The girl was sitting bolt upright in her chair, her hands clutching at its arms, her face deadly pale.

"What is it?" asked Mrs. Fittleworth, crossing over to her.

"Oh—it can't be," said Winnie in a low voice, half choking. "He couldn't have done it—I know he couldn't have done it."

"What—do you know him?" asked the Canon anxiously.

The girl nodded.

"If it's the same—Mr. Grayson. Yes. He was at the Art School with me. And I've seen him since. I—I know him quite well. It's impossible. Oh, oughtn't I to tell the police? It's dreadful to think of."

Mrs. Fittleworth, who noticed the deep blush to which the girl's ashy cheeks had given place, with a motherly instinct put her arm over her shoulder.

"Don't worry, dear," she said. "The Canon has said the police don't necessarily suspect him. If he is really the Mr. Grayson you know—and he may not be, after all—of course he will be able to explain. You're quite done up with all this terrible affair, and I'm going to take you to bed. Come along."

"Thank you," said Winnie gratefully, "you are kind to me. I'm very silly, I know, but I can't bear to think that he—he is suspected. I know he couldn't have done it."

"Of course he couldn't," said Mrs. Fittleworth soothingly. "Now—I must insist. You come to bed, dear."

When the Canon himself went to bed that night he had to listen to a little lecture. And he took it calmly—from force of habit—much more calmly than if it had come from the Dean, or even the Bishop. Whereat it is evident that even for cathedral dignitaries there is a higher court than the mere ecclesiastical.

"Really, Charles," said his wife, "you ought to have noticed that the poor girl had gone through quite enough for one day."

The Canon tried defensive argument, which was foolish of him—for he ought to have remembered that he never succeeded.

"But how was I to know, my dear, that she was acquainted with the young man?"

"Oh, do be reasonable, Charles. You ought not to have mentioned the subject of the murder at all at that time of night. Doris and I had been doing our best to get the girl's mind off it. And then you came in and started it all again!"

"Why didn't you stop me, my dear?"

"Stop you!" exclaimed his wife; "stop you when you once begin to hold forth on a subject. How can anyone stop you? *I* can't. There. I know you didn't mean to upset her, but you ought to have thought."

"I suppose I ought," said the Canon resignedly. "I'm very sorry. Good night, my dear."

CHAPTER IX.
The Cigar Band

The crowd that had assembled at the inquest at Marsh Quay loitered for a while discussing the one important topic. Newspaper men were busy with notebook and camera. The removal of the body of Reginald Templeton from the "Mariner's Arms" to the mortuary at Frattenbury, pending the funeral the next day, was eagerly watched. Members of the jury, for the most part stolid agricultural labourers or boatmen, were closely questioned by friends or relatives, but, on the whole, recognising the importance of their office, were not communicative.

Mr. Proctor refused to say a word to anyone. He came out of the "Mariner's Arms," lighting a cigar as he did so, and walked straight over to his house opposite, blandly smiling at an irrepressible reporter who asked him to pose for his camera.

The coroner drove away with the Chief Constable in the latter's car, austere and grave as usual. Anthony Crosby, the superintendent and Colson held a brief consultation in the inn parlour, where it was arranged that the lawyer should call at the police station the next morning for further discussion.

"What are you going to do, Colson?" asked the superintendent as he rose to go. "Are you coming back to Frattenbury?"

"I want to think a bit, sir. I may cycle in later on. But I'm fairly puzzled just now. There are two men we want to get hold of, anyhow—this artist chap who was staying here, and Moss, opposite."

The superintendent nodded.

"We're bound to do that," he said. "I expect there'll be reports when I get back to the station. Well, I'll leave you now."

Everyone else but the detective having left the inn, Mrs. Yates locked the front door and came into the bar parlour.

"Is there anything I can do for you, Mr. Colson?"

"Yes, please. I should like some strong tea. Then I want you to keep everyone away."

"Trust me for that, sir. Not a soul comes into this house till six, when I'm bound to open. I want to have a little quiet myself, Mr. Colson. What with all these reporters and people asking questions I'm fairly bewildered. I hope there won't be any more murders here as long as I keeps the 'Mariner's Arms,' I do indeed."

Seated at the table, drinking his tea, his notebook in front of him, Detective-Sergeant Colson deliberately and methodically reviewed the case, making his deductions as he did so, and writing them out concisely. And this was the result when he finally closed his pocket-book:

"*Templeton's object in coming to Marsh Quay.* First, to see Moss. That requires investigation. Secondly, to see his cousin. We know all about that. Thirdly, an interview with some unknown person in Frattenbury, who must have been the last person who saw him before he was murdered. Why did not that person come forward to give evidence? But he might not have lived in Frattenbury itself—
—he might have spoken, loosely, of the neighbourhood. He might have arranged to see Moss again—or this artist chap—or even Proctor. They are all possible.

"*Reason for appointment.* He hinted that he was carrying something valuable. We know what that was. Diamonds. There were probably more than the one we found. Who has them now?

"*Clues.* Only four at present of any value—possibly only two. (1) The blotting-paper. Not easy to make out. If deciphered, it might lead to finding out with whom the appointment was made, or what it was about. But very uncertain. (2) The diamond. But that only appears to prove that he had others. (3) The walking-stick. Most important, this. It is pretty certain that the man who thinks he has recovered it is the criminal. If only I hadn't muddled it! (4) The cigar band. I ought to have spotted that, and not have left it to that confounded parson to find. There may be something in it, certainly.

"*Possible suspects.* (1) Moss. Why did he leave in such a hurry? The fact of the murderer being on the spot last night, when he got that walking-stick, seems to rule Moss out. But not necessarily. He might easily have run down from London last night. There's a lot to be inquired into here. (2) Grayson, the artist. Why did he leave in a hurry? He's certainly got to be run to earth. (3) Proctor. Yes—Proctor puzzles me. Such a cool old chap! He would have known exactly where to land in that canoe—and, if so, he knew perfectly well that the boy would find it there in the morning. Also, he's been in Switzerland. That stick again! And I thought he was never going to leave off examining that cigar band at the inquest. We must keep a sharp eye on Proctor. If he's not simply a fool, he's as wily as they make 'em."

When he had closed his notebook and put it in his pocket, the detective lighted his pipe and sat, smoking thoughtfully, looking out of the window. He realised that the case was all the more difficult because the few clues that he held, and the slight facts he had to go upon, might equally apply to any one of the three persons he had enumerated as being suspicious. And if, as it seemed, his work was to eliminate two of these persons, he was anxious to make no mistake.

Colson was not the detective of fiction. He was simply a shrewd, careful man, keenly observant, with a police training. Had he been that brilliant genius which the writer of fiction is so fond of delineating, he would, after his manner, by this time have made some supernaturally clever deduction, which would have enabled him to spot the criminal at once, and to run him down unerringly, with the additional triumph attached to it that all his colleagues, and every other person concerned, had been absolutely wrong in their suspicions. He would, probably, have adopted extraordinary disguises, kept all his clues and methods to himself, and never have given a hint of them to his superior officers, and finally have achieved that superlative climax in which he would have exclaimed, "Alone I did it!"

But Colson was what, in spite of the writers of fiction, is a useful personage in tracing crime—Colson was a policeman, and he knew the value of those often-derided police methods. He, for example, could sit now, calmly smoking his pipe, secure in the knowledge that every police station in the district was on the look-out for Grayson, the artist, that in a very short time Moss would probably be found—also by police methods—and that a little police machinery, which the superintendent was already putting in hand as a result of their brief conference after the inquest, would prevent Proctor from slipping away from the neighbourhood unobserved—if he had any such idea in his mind.

As Colson looked out of the window, half lost in reflections, he noticed a man detach himself from the little group that still lingered near the scene of the tragedy, and go walking up the quay, hands in pockets. It was Tom Gale, the "crew and cook" of the schooner that was still moored at the quay head, waiting for his cargo.

An idea struck the detective.

"That chap was about all the time," he argued, "it might be worth while having another chat with him."

So he went out, strolled along the quay, and finally stepped aboard the schooner, where he found Tom Gale in his favourite attitude of leaning over the bulwarks.

"Well," he said, as he went up to him, "you gave your evidence well to-day, my man. We like a witness who speaks out plainly, and you did it."

Tom grinned approval of the compliment. Inwardly he was proud of being in any way mixed up with the case. He knew he could tell the story—with self-complimentary embellishments—for many weeks in divers bars, and that many invitations to "have one with me, mate," would be the resulting homage.

"Ah," he said, "I told 'em what I knew. I wish it had been more, sir."

"So do we all. But what you told us of Templeton crossing the estuary—and seeing Moss—was important, you know."

Tom Gale made a mental note of how he could truthfully say afterwards that if it hadn't been for him the police would have missed the very essence of things—the detective himself had told him so—and then spoke.

"Ah," he said, "I seen him plain enough. Just over yonder 'twas," and he jerked his thumb in the direction of the opposite shore, "that 'ere little Jew fellow, Moss, he stood on the shore, just there. D'ye think 'twas him as did it, sir?" he asked with relish.

The detective shook his head mysteriously.

"Ah," he said, "we mustn't jump to conclusions hastily, you know. So you saw him plainly, did you?"

"Ah. T'other chap was only just a-askin' on me who lived in that house and I was tellin' on him, when there was Moss himself—I pointed 'im out."

"What do you mean by 't'other chap'?" asked the detective sharply.

"Why, him as was standin' just where you might be, sir, at the time—that young artist feller what was lodging at the 'Mariner's Arms.'"

"Oh!" said Colson, thoughtfully, "he was with you, was he?"

"O' course he was, sir—now, ought I to ha' told 'em that at the inquest? I never thought of it."

"No, no," said the other. "It didn't matter at all. But, tell me. If this artist—Grayson is his name—was with you, did he recognise Mr. Templeton when he came back? Or speak to him?"

Tom Gale shook his head.

"No, sir; directly Mr. Templeton started coming across, this here artist chap went straight back to the inn—looked almost as if he didn't want Mr. Templeton to see him."

"Oh, did it?" said Colson. "Yes, I see."

He filled his pipe and handed his pouch to the other man. Tom Gale put his hand in his pocket, ostensibly to get his pipe, and exclaimed:

"'Ullo. I'd forgotten this," and drew forth a crumpled cigar.

He looked at it ruefully.

"Meant to ha' smoked him yesterday, bein' Sunday," he said; "now he's too far gone. I must chop him up and smoke him in my pipe. 'Tain't often I gets hold of a cigar, guv'nor."

Colson, who was looking at the cigar intently, asked him quietly:

"Where did you get it from?"

"That 'ere artist feller we was just a-talkin' about gave 'im to me, sir, up yonder in the 'Mariner's Arms.' A good 'un, I reckon, ain't he?"

The detective took the cigar in his hand and smelt it. But, all the time, he was carefully examining the band.

"Yes, it's good enough," he said. "Pity you've spoilt it. Oh—so Grayson gave it to you, did he?"

"Yes, sir—Saturday afternoon, we was sittin' in the bar parlour, me and him, and he gave 'im to me. He smoked two of 'em while I was there."

"Well, look here," said Colson, "have one of mine instead, to make up for it." And he pulled out what he called his "diplomatic cigar case." He rarely smoked anything but a pipe himself, but he always kept a few good cigars in his pocket. He knew their value—when he was in search of information.

"Take a couple," he went on.

"Thankee, sir—don't mind if I do."

Tom Gale lighted one of them and smoked complacently. The detective talked volubly and then bid him good afternoon.

"Blowed if he ain't took that cigar o' mine with him," murmured Tom Gale after he had gone. "Absent-minded like, I'll 'low. It doan't matter, though."

Colson, who had quietly slipped the crushed cigar into his pocket, walked rapidly back to the inn. Arrived in the bar parlour, he laid the cigar on the table, took from his case the band which the Canon had handed in at the inquest, and carefully compared it with the other.

A smile lightened his face.

"That's better!" he exclaimed. "Here's something to go upon at last. The same brand, that's what they are. It's a good brand, but not specially exclusive as that idiot of a parson wanted to make out. Same brand as he smoked, he said. Very likely, but the clergy ain't got the monopoly of the cigar trade. Anyhow, this looks convincing. This young Grayson smoked these cigars, and someone who was aboard the yacht smoked one of 'em there. It's good enough to go upon. Mrs. Yates!"

He opened the door as he spoke. The landlady bustled in.

"I'm going back to Frattenbury now. And I shan't be staying the night here."

"Sorry to lose you, Mr. Colson."

"Can't be helped, Mrs. Yates. I don't think there's anything to keep me here for the present. Oh—tell me. This young lodger of yours smoked cigars, didn't he?"

"He did, sir—as I knows. He was always dropping the ash about—on my bedroom carpet too."

"Do your carpets good, if you rub the ash in."

"Lor', sir! And the mess he made in the grate, too."

The detective looked at the grate sharply. On the top of the coals, that were laid there ready to be lighted, was a sprinkling of cigar ash and a couple of red and gold bands. He picked them out.

"These came off his cigars, I suppose?"

"They must have, Mr. Colson. It's few folks ever smokes them things here. Pipes and 'baccy is what they mostly uses."

"Quite so. Well, I'll run up and pack my bag while you get my bill ready."

He rode quickly into Frattenbury, in a very cheerful mood, and reported to the superintendent. That functionary was delighted.

"Good!" he exclaimed. "You've done well, Colson. We must have this Grayson at any price. Thompson has just been in to report that he stayed at Selham on Sunday and Sunday night—at the 'Wheatsheaf.' "

"Did he?" exclaimed Colson. "That makes matters clearer than ever. He was on the spot on Sunday night, eh?"

"He was seen riding into Frattenbury a couple of hours ago," went on the superintendent. "We'll soon have him. He can't get away by train—we've seen to that. By the way, Colson, the post has just brought in a letter from the London police about Moss. You'd better see it."

He handed a typewritten paper to the detective, who read:

Isaac Moss. In reference to your inquiries concerning this man, I beg to report as follows. He rents a small office at 13a, Hatton Garden. Deals in jewels, mostly diamonds, and is well known. Private residence, "Fairview," No. 53, Compton Avenue, Brondesbury. Nothing known against him. Possesses passport, as he is frequently in Amsterdam. Boats being watched as precaution.

"I sent Tyler up yesterday," went on the superintendent. "He's probably on his track by this time."

Late that night a message came through from Tyler:

Tracked our man, and have him under observation.

Colson smoked the pipe of peace at his own fireside that night. His wife listened attentively as he told her all that he had done that day.

"Looks promising, doesn't it?"

She thought for a minute or two before she replied:

"I hope so—for your sake. But there are still difficulties. I want to know why the little bag with the one diamond was put back in Mr. Templeton's waistcoat pocket—if the rest were stolen. And you say yourself that the cigar band was not a *very* extraordinary one.

Be careful, dear, won't you? I want you to come out of this well, you know——"

Colson smiled grimly.

"All right, old girl," he said, "I'll be careful. I know what you mean. We don't want to get anyone sent up for trial till we're quite certain. It's too big a risk—and I'm not taking any risks in this job."

CHAPTER X.
Harold Grayson is Detained

Harold Grayson came down to breakfast on the Tuesday morning in the little cottage where he had found a lodging in the downland village of Linderton, some four or five miles north of Frattenbury, profoundly oblivious of the fact that the stolid-looking policeman who was digging in his garden directly opposite his lodgings had been, according to orders, watching the house all night and was yawning heavily at the prospect of the snooze he would take when the promised relief came that morning.

For although Harold Grayson had escaped detection for the moment by riding round Frattenbury instead of through it on his way to the downs, the net which the superintendent had quietly spread had soon closed in upon him. That stolid village policeman, Constable Drake, to wit, already had a description of the fugitive in his pocket, and when Grayson had alighted from his bicycle the evening before and asked him where he could get a bed, Drake had recognised the quarry at once.

But Drake was absolutely imperturbable. By never a sign did he intimate that anything unusual was happening. Instead, he tilted back his helmet, scratched his head thoughtfully—for he was really thinking astutely all the time—and said:

"A bed, sir? Well, there's the 'Blue Lion,' but I'm not sure if you'd like it. It ain't up to much"—that was because the "Blue Lion" was at the extreme end of the village, well away from the constable's cottage. "Let me see, now. Tell you what, sir. We don't often have anyone stayin' here, but there's a neighbour o' mine who lets rooms sometimes—clean and comfortable they are. You come along o' me, sir, and I'll do what I can for you."

With a view to his own as well as the artist's comfort, he led him straightway to the cottage opposite his own, and, with bland persuasion, induced the occupant to take in the stranger. Grayson, as he unstrapped his holdall from his bicycle, gratefully gave him a tip, which the policeman as gratefully acknowledged.

"Tell you what, sir," he said, "Mrs. Goring ain't got much room for your bicycle. There's my shed handy. You can put it there if you like."

Which Grayson promptly did, and as soon as he had departed Drake promptly removed the valves—with much satisfaction. Then he went indoors, slowly and laboriously wrote a letter, which began, "While on duty at 6.38 p.m. in the main road at Linderton I was accosted," and dispatched it by his son, who took it into Frattenbury on his bicycle and brought out a reply.

That is all that is necessary to say about Police-Constable Drake. When he got his well-earned snooze he had a vision of sergeant's stripes in the future.

As Grayson ate his eggs and bacon he could see the line of downs opposite and was picturing in his mind a pleasant day's work, when a smart motor-car drew up at the garden gate of the cottage and a tall, military-looking man got out of it, followed by a stiff-looking man in plain clothes, who took up his position outside the cottage. A moment later the landlady opened the door of the room and announced:

"A gentleman to see you, sir."

Grayson rose, surprised.

"Good morning," exclaimed the newcomer. "Your name is Grayson, I believe—Mr. Harold Grayson?"

"It is," replied Grayson; "but I confess I haven't the honour——"

"I am Major Renshaw, Chief Constable of this district. I fear I have rather an unpleasant duty to perform."

"Yes?"

"You were recently staying at the 'Mariner's Arms' at Marsh Quay, I believe?"

Grayson, looking a little uncomfortable under the penetrating gaze of Major Renshaw, replied that he was.

"And you left rather suddenly, very early on Sunday morning?"

"I did—but I don't understand——"

"It was a little unfortunate, Mr. Grayson, that you did so. Please understand that I am making no charge against you at present, but I suppose you are aware what took place at Marsh Quay the night before you left?"

The young man shook his head.

"I don't know what you mean," he replied.

"Oh, come now!" said Major Renshaw sharply. "Mr. Templeton's murder—you must have heard of it. Everyone's talking about it, and you've been in the neighbourhood all the time."

"Mr. Templeton's murder?" stammered Grayson. "He—he had his yacht there."

"I see you know *that*," said the Chief Constable grimly. "And do you mean to tell me you don't know that he was murdered on that yacht?"

"I—I—really I don't."

Major Renshaw shrugged his shoulders.

"Perhaps you can explain," he said coldly. "You must be an extraordinary young man either to think you can make me believe you know nothing or to have escaped hearing about it. Perhaps you won't mind telling me your movements since you left Marsh Quay?"

"I—I can do that. You may not believe me, and I admit it sounds strange—but I'll tell you the facts. I left the 'Mariner's Arms' quite early, intending to go to Frattenbury. Then I changed my mind and went to Selham. I put up at the 'Wheatsheaf' there. I asked them to give me some lunch to take out with me—I wanted to do some sketching—I am fond of being alone—I suffered from shell-shock in the war—and I find it rests me."

"Go on," said the Major, a little more sympathetically now that Grayson had touched on his erstwhile profession. "What did you do next?"

"I found my way to a very lonely bit of the coast and sketched. I can show you the sketches. I particularly wanted to get a sunset effect, so I waited till then. When I started back I began to feel hungry, and called at a solitary farm-house, where they gave me bread and cheese and milk. It was dark when I left and I wandered considerably out of my way before I got back to the 'Wheatsheaf.' When I did, I was awfully tired. I glanced in the tap-room. There was a noisy crowd there, so I went straight to bed. I never spoke to anyone."

"Go on, please. The next morning?"

"I was up early. There was only a girl about, and she got me some breakfast. Then I paid my bill and rode off."

"Where?"

"To the lower part of the estuary. I bought some food at a grocer's shop in a village I passed through, sketched till the afternoon, and then rode out here. With the exception of the girl in the morning and a deaf old woman in the grocer's shop, I never spoke to a soul all day till I asked the village policeman here where I could get a bed. Those are the facts, Major Renshaw. I hope you don't dispute them?"

The Chief Constable regarded him critically, but did not answer his question. Instead he asked:

"Did you know this Mr. Reginald Templeton?"

The young man hesitated a little.

"Yes—I did," he admitted.

"Did you see him to speak to at Marsh Quay?"

"N—no."

"You knew he was there—you have admitted that already."

"Yes—I knew he was there."

"You avoided him, then?"

Grayson nodded.

"Why?"

"Well—you see—we weren't exactly friends. That's why I came away. I didn't want to meet him."

"Why?"

After a brief silence the Chief Constable said:

"Well, Mr. Grayson, I told you mine was an unpleasant duty. I make no charge against you at present, but there are certain ugly facts which you will have to account for. You are not under arrest—or I should not, of course, have questioned you—but I am afraid I shall have to ask you to come back with me to Frattenbury and I must warn you that you will be detained there, at all events till you can give a further account of yourself. I am sorry if there is any mistake. I cannot say more."

Grayson bowed. He was still very pale and a little agitated. He recognised the seriousness of his position.

"I understand," he said quietly, "and of course I cannot refuse to go with you; but I assure you it is all a mistake."

"I hope it is," said Major Renshaw dryly. "You had better bring some things with you—for your own comfort."

Just before they were ready to start the Chief Constable suddenly said:

"Have you any cigars on you, Mr. Grayson?"

The young man pulled out his case.

"These are all I have left. Why?"

"Thank you," said Major Renshaw, putting the case in his pocket. "I'm afraid I must deprive you of them."

"Am I not allowed to smoke?" asked Grayson. "I understood I was not under arrest."

Major Renshaw smiled grimly, and as soon as they were in the car offered his cigarette-case.

"Smoke, by all means," he said. "I'll supply you willingly. Only we rather bar cigars."

He looked at him keenly as he spoke. But Grayson was lighting a cigarette quite calmly.

When they arrived at the police station a further examination took place in the presence of the superintendent and Colson. Grayson, who had recovered his equanimity by this time, repeated all he had told the Chief Constable. The superintendent took careful notes.

"We shall make inquiries, Mr. Grayson," he said, "to verify these statements so far as the people to whom you say you spoke are concerned. Now will you tell me, please, something about yourself?"

"In what way?"

"Well, your home."

"I am at present in lodgings in London. I will give you the address. My home is just outside Marlow, in Buckinghamshire. My father, who is a county magistrate, is well known—Mr. Osmond Grayson."

"What are you doing in this neighbourhood?"

"Sketching, mostly."

"Did you know that Mr. Templeton was likely to be at Marsh Quay?"

"Certainly not. I have already told you I wished to avoid him when I found he was there."

"Why?"

"Because—well, the whole affair is a private matter."

"You need not tell us unless you wish to, Mr. Grayson," interposed the Chief Constable. "But if the rest of your story is correct it will materially help us to account for your hasty departure."

"Very well," said the young man after a moment's thought, "there is really nothing to conceal. Some years ago my father was involved in a lawsuit with Mr. Templeton—and won it. Templeton had to sell his estate to pay the costs, and my father bought it. He hated the lot of us, and, I think, justly, because it's always been my opinion that my father was not so much in the right as the law said he was. My father knows I think this. Well, if you want the truth, when I knew that Templeton was at Marsh Quay I didn't want him to see me, because I'm a bit ashamed of the whole affair. I watched to see him come off the yacht to make quite sure it was he, and when I saw it was, I made up my mind to leave early the next morning. That's all there is in it."

The superintendent nodded thoughtfully.

"You don't happen to know the name of Mr. Templeton's solicitors when this case was tried, I suppose?"

"Yes, I do. Of course I remember. Sir Henry Cateford was his counsel—I forget the name of the junior—and his solicitors were Crosby and Paxton, well-known people, I believe."

The Chief Constable and the superintendent exchanged glances, but Colson broke in at that moment. "Do you recognise this cigar?" he asked, showing him the crushed one he had received from Tom Gale.

Grayson examined it.

"It's the same brand I've been smoking lately," he said. "I couldn't swear, of course, that it's one of my actual cigars. What of it? If I can explain anything I'm quite willing to do so."

"Can you tell us if you smoked one of your cigars on board Mr. Templeton's yacht, then?" asked Colson.

"I never was on his yacht. Why do you ask?"

The detective did not reply to this. He asked another question:

"Can you account for your movements from ten o'clock on Saturday night to, say, six o'clock on the following morning?"

"No, I can't," replied Grayson.

"Why not?"

"Because I happened to be asleep. I went to bed at the 'Mariner's Arms' just before ten, and I woke up at a quarter-past six. I can't help you there."

"It was to help you that the question was asked," said the superintendent gravely.

The young man gave a short laugh.

"I see what you mean," he said, "but the same thing applies to a score or so of people who were sleeping close to the quay that night, doesn't it? I can't prove an alibi any more than they can."

The Chief Constable shrugged his shoulders, but would not commit himself.

"Well, Mr. Grayson," he said, "thank you for all you have told us. I'm sorry we must detain you for a time, but I hope, for your sake, it will not be long. Superintendent Norton will do his best to make you comfortable. We shan't lock you up in a cell, you know—unless we see cause to arrest you. But you won't be allowed to leave the house."

"Well?" he asked when Grayson was out of the room.

"I'm not satisfied yet," said Colson. "There's that matter of the cigar band. I'd like to have it identified by Canon Fittleworth. I don't expect it, but he *may* help us there."

The superintendent laughed.

"Don't be too down on the parson, Colson," he said. "We'll see what he says by and by. Meanwhile, Mr. Crosby ought to be here. He can identify Grayson's statement about the lawsuit, sir."

"Yes," said the Chief Constable, "I agree."

A few minutes later Crosby came in, by appointment, and was told of the detention of Grayson and the statement he had made.

"I can verify all he says about there being ill-feeling between my late client and Grayson's family," he said. "That's perfectly true. I don't know this young Grayson personally, but from what I've heard of him he's all right. He did splendidly in the war, I know—and he's had to pay for it—yes—shell-shock, Major. That's all right. As to what you tell me about the cigar band, you'll get Canon Fittleworth to identify it, I suppose? Exactly. As it's a fairly well-known brand, I shouldn't think there's much upon which to build a case; but that's your lookout. Whoever the fellow is, I hope you'll get him. Now, I'm returning to London immediately after the funeral. I shall come down to the adjourned inquest, of course. But is there anything else I ought to know?"

"We're in confidence, Mr. Crosby?" asked the wary superintendent.

"Of course. As the legal representative of the deceased I shall naturally observe that."

"We'd like to show you a few things we found in the cabin, then. Colson, where are they?"

Colson, who had stipulated that at this juncture no mention should be made of the walking-stick—he was emphatic on this point—produced the chamois leather bag, the diamond and the blotting-pad. From the latter he had transcribed the scraps of writing, in print capitals, onto a piece of ordinary paper.

The lawyer looked at the exhibits shrewdly.

"Wonder what he was doing with diamonds," he said. "Of course there were more than this one. And the bag was not tied up, you say? H'm—queer! Yes—I see—the first letter you've put together very well. Evidently his appointment with Moss. You've got your eye on him, eh?"

"One of us will probably run up to interview him to-morrow," said the superintendent. "He's under observation."

"Of course—good. And this other bit of writing—— Gad! it's a poser, isn't it? Have you made it out?"

"Not yet," said Colson.

"I'll take a copy. I'm rather keen on this sort of thing. I'll see what I can make of it. Of course, as you say, it might be of importance—if in any way it put you on the track of the individual with whom Templeton had an appointment on Saturday night." He copied it carefully. "You've allowed for the blank spaces in the original?" he asked Colson.

"Yes."

The lawyer studied the letters for a minute.

a d ver zr ice s o ion & roo
s is nal

"There's one point about it that strikes one," he said. "I dare say you've noticed it, sergeant. There aren't many words that have the letters ZR close together. The only one I can think of is 'Ezra,' eh?"

"I thought of that, too, sir."

The superintendent was looking over the lawyer's shoulder. He laughed.

"Ezra's ices!" he exclaimed. "Sounds like an Italian Jew and an ice-cream barrow!"

CHAPTER XI.
The Canon's Cigars

One can only suppose that the morbid curiosity which always attracts a crowd of people to the burial of a suicide or victim of a murder repays the onlookers in some sense or other. It is difficult to say how it does so. The utmost they see or hear is a glimpse of an ordinary coffin and the words of the Burial Service.

It was a large crowd that gathered on the Tuesday afternoon to witness the funeral of Reginald Templeton, which took place in the cemetery a mile out of Frattenbury. There were few mourners. The Canon's brother, a retired colonel, had run down for the occasion and occupied the leading mourning coach with the Canon himself and Winnie Cotterill. Crosby and the doctor who had attended the case came in the other.

On the return journey to the city, Winnie Cotterill, who was seated next to the Canon, remarked:

"It's a curious thing, Canon Fittleworth, but several times I've had the impression that Frattenbury is familiar to me."

"Really?"

"Yes," said the girl. "It's just come over me now. That view of the Cathedral spire—and the little stream of water we've just crossed—it's just as if I've seen them before."

"Perhaps you have," said the Canon.

The girl shook her head.

"I don't see how I can," she replied; "I've never been here before, so far as I know."

"Well, you see," said the Canon, with a little pride, "our Cathedral is pretty well known, and I dare say you've seen pictures or photographs of it. That might account for it."

"Perhaps," replied Winnie slowly, "but it doesn't seem to—it's that funny sort of feeling that I've been here, don't you know?"

"Yes, I know," said Canon Fittleworth, "it's a psychological curiosity. I've had it myself often. 'There are more things in heaven and earth—' eh, Charles?"

"True. Possibly," he went on to the girl, "you've heard people describing Frattenbury."

She laughed.

"I'm afraid you'll think me very ignorant," she said, "but I don't think I ever heard of Frattenbury till I read about the murder in the paper yesterday morning. I've never even been in the South of England."

"We're not so famous as we thought we were, Miss Cotterill," said the Canon with a smile. "What do you think of our War Memorial?"

They were passing through a little square just at the entry of the city, in the centre of which stood one of those, now familiar, erections which are to remind people that the Great European War was characterised by many atrocities.

She looked at it, shrugged her shoulders—it may have been the expression of an opinion—and then, closing her eyes, said slowly:

"It looks as if there ought to be a big lamp-post there, instead."

"There was," replied the Canon dryly. "I don't know that I didn't prefer it. Really, Miss Cotterill, you must have considerable psychic powers."

"I never knew it till now."

A minute or two later they entered the Cathedral precincts, and drew up at the Canon's residence. As they got out Mr. Norwood happened to be passing. He raised his hat and bowed in his stiff, formal manner. Winnie Cotterill looked at him intently.

"Who was that?" she asked the Canon as they went into the house.

"One of our Frattenbury solicitors—a Mr. Norwood," replied the Canon.

"It's that queer sensation again," remarked the girl. "When he took his hat off it seemed to me exactly as if I'd seen him before—only that he's older or something."

"Well, it's quite possible. Although he's lived all his life in Frattenbury he's often in London. One really meets—quite casually—many people who leave an impression on one."

"I suppose it's that," said Winnie. "It must be—of course."

"Is his name familiar to you?"

"Not a bit. I never heard it before."

There were several letters for the Canon lying on the hall table. He took them up, saying as he did so:

"Tea ought to be ready. I expect you'll find Mrs. Fittleworth in the drawing-room. Do you mind telling her I'll be there in a minute?"

She hesitated.

"Canon Fittleworth?"

"Yes."

"If you *can* find out whether the police have done anything—about Mr. Grayson—before I go, I should be so grateful."

"I will," he said. "I'll go round to the police station immediately after tea."

"It's awfully good of you."

He nodded and smiled.

"Don't worry," he said.

Then, as she went into the drawing-room, he opened his letters. His face looked grave as he read one of them, a note from the police superintendent.

Dear Sir,

We have detained, on suspicion, the young artist, named Grayson, who was staying at the "Mariner's Arms" at Marsh Quay. I shall be grateful if you can kindly make it convenient to call here any time between five and six this afternoon. We want you to corroborate a small matter. I called this morning, but you were out, and I was told you would not be disengaged till after the funeral. Will you kindly bring with you one of your cigars similar to that which you say contained the band found by you at Marsh Quay?

- *Yours faithfully,*
- *Thomas Norton.*

He thought for a moment, and then went into his study and rang the bell.

"Tell your mistress I want to see her for a minute," he told the maid.

"My dear," he said to his wife when she came in, "the police have written to tell me they have that young man, Grayson, detained at the police station. I had only just promised Miss Cotterill to go round after tea and make inquiries, before she leaves. I shall have to go in any case. They've asked me."

"Poor child," said Mrs. Fittleworth, "she seems very much concerned about Mr. Grayson. I think she's fond of him, Charles. I *hope* he isn't the murderer."

The Canon shrugged his shoulders.

"That's not for us to judge," he said, "nor must we jump at hasty conclusions. If there's nothing against him, however, I should like to be able to tell Miss Cotterill before she goes." He looked at his watch. "Her train leaves in less than an hour—and they may keep me at the police station longer than I thought."

Mrs. Fittleworth, out of the kindness of her heart, rose to the occasion.

"She shall stay another night. I'll persuade her. I like the girl very much, Charles. You see, if there's nothing really against the young man we ought to know in the morning. And if there *is*, well, perhaps I can comfort her a little."

The Canon beamed his satisfaction.

"I quite agree," he said. "Don't tell her just now that the police have detained him."

"Don't *you* let it out, dear!" she replied. "Give me five minutes to persuade her to stay, and then come in to tea."

Left to himself, Canon Fittleworth opened his cigar cupboard and took out a box. He was about to place one of the three or four remaining cigars in his case, when he stopped.

"Yes," he murmured, "I'll take the box itself round. I ought to have thought of that before. It may be useful!"

After tea he went round to the police station and was shown into the superintendent's private office, where he found, with that functionary, Major Renshaw and Colson.

"Sorry to give you the trouble, Canon," said Major Renshaw, "but we've detained this young man on suspicion, and you may help us. So far, I'm bound to admit, he's given a straightforward account of himself. His story sounded a little thin at first, but we've corroborated it as far as we were able. Only, there's one point that is dead against him. And that's where *you* come in."

"What is that?" asked the Canon.

The Chief Constable nodded to Colson to go on.

"Well, sir," said the detective, "you produced, at the inquest, yesterday, a cigar band which you stated you found in Mr. Templeton's cabin."

"I did."

"You would recognise it again?"

"Most certainly. I said, you remember, that it was the same brand as my own cigars."

The detective smiled pityingly.

"That may be," he said with a touch of sarcasm in his voice; "at all events we want you to tell us now—is this the band?"

And he took from his pocket-case the band which had figured at the inquest. The Canon took a quick glance at it.

"No. Certainly not!" he exclaimed.

The three men looked at him in surprise. Colson ejaculated:

"Great Scott!"

Then he said:

"Come, sir—it *must* be."

"I tell you it isn't. It's entirely different. The band I found in the cabin, and handed in yesterday afternoon, was similar to these."

And he opened his own cigar box.

"But *this* is the band you handed in yesterday, sir," exclaimed Colson, pointing to the one he had just produced.

"It is nothing of the kind," said the Canon a little hotly. "I am ready to swear to that."

There was a moment or two of intense silence, and then the superintendent said to Colson:

"Are you *sure* this is the band you received from the inquest?"

Colson, who, like the Canon, did not relish his integrity being shaken, replied stiffly:

"Quite sure, sir. I saw the Canon lay it on the table, an——"

"But you didn't examine it closely then," broke in the Canon.

"No—but I watched it being passed from man to man of the jury, and when it was finally put down on the table I didn't remove my eyes from it till it was in my hands."

The superintendent slowly nodded his head.

"You are quite certain, Canon?" he asked again.

"Absolutely. This is *not* the band I laid on the table."

Colson gave a low whistle and then pursed up his lips.

"There *may* be an explanation," he said, "and a very significant one, too. But it is most important that these facts do not get about. May we rely on your discretion, Canon Fittleworth?"

"Decidedly. Of course I shall say nothing."

"Well—the point is this, Canon Fittleworth. Now that you know so much I may as well tell you. This young Grayson was smoking a brand of cigars similar to that off which this particular band, which you repudiate, came. You will admit it was damning evidence against him."

"It certainly was," said the Canon. "I am only too glad to have helped to clear an innocent man."

"Yes," said the Chief Constable thoughtfully, "I suppose—I suppose this clears him—but——"

Colson, who had sprung to his feet suddenly, interrupted him.

"Wait a bit," he exclaimed, "I'll make still more certain. Can I borrow your motor-bike sir?" he asked the superintendent. "I'll be back in twenty minutes—or less."

The superintendent nodded.

"All right, Colson."

"I'll wait till he comes back," said the Canon. "I am anxious, for certain reasons, to see this young man set at liberty before I go home."

"I'm glad you're staying," said the superintendent, who was examining one of the Canon's cigars. "I want to have a talk with you about this. I see what you mean. This is a brand I don't know at all."

"I don't suppose you do," replied the Canon. "They are not on the market. A Spanish friend of mine sent them me direct from Cuba. They're something very special."

"Why didn't you say this at the inquest, sir?"

The Canon hesitated.

"Well—er—I really was so very much taken aback at Norwood's manner—I am not accustomed to be spoken to like that—in public. And it made me forget what I should otherwise have said."

Again the superintendent addressed him in sorrowful rebuke:

"Oh, Canon Fittleworth! You really *ought* to have told the jury—or even if you forgot it at that moment, you *might* have told us. See the trouble to which you have put us."

The worthy Canon bristled a little.

"Why didn't you come to me?" he asked.

"Well—sir—when we saw what sort of a brand it was, fairly ordinary, we didn't think it worth while."

"Ah," said the Canon, a twinkle in his eye now, "see the trouble you have given yourselves! If you'd only remembered that I *said* it was a particular brand!"

"Come, Canon," interposed the Chief Constable with a laugh, "we mustn't get acrimonious about it. It's a little mistake on both sides. But now what you've got to do is to try to remember if anyone else but yourself smoked cigars taken from that box."

"Certainly," replied the Canon, "I can remember at the moment someone who took a cigar out of my box."

"Who was it?" asked the Chief Constable eagerly.

"You yourself, Renshaw—last time you dined with me. And you remarked what an excellent smoke it was."

"Ha, ha, ha," laughed the Chief Constable. "You want to fix the murder on *me*, eh?"

The Canon joined in the laugh.

"Circumstantial evidence, eh?" he said.

"But, seriously, Canon," went on Major Renshaw, "I don't expect you to do it now, but I do ask you to shut yourself up in your study and make a big effort of memory. It's wonderful how one can recall little details if one really tries. Write out the names of everyone— *everyone* mind—even the most unlikely persons—to whom you remember you offered a cigar out of that box. And if you can call to mind anybody who took away a cigar out of your house without smoking it, that will be *most* important."

"Very well," replied the Canon, "I'll do what you suggest. My circle of friends is a fairly respectable one, however, and I hope I don't number a murderer among them."

Meanwhile Colson had rushed over to Marsh Quay. It was not yet six o'clock, so the inn was not open. He knocked at the door and Mrs. Yates let him in. Satisfying himself that there was no one else about, he said to her:

"As I told you before, Mrs. Yates, I look upon you as an exceedingly discreet woman. Now, I want you to keep your mouth shut about what I'm going to ask you."

"I will, Mr. Colson."

"You've got a good memory, eh?"

"I hope so, sir."

"Well, try and remember now. This young man who was lodging with you, what did his luggage consist of?"

"It was placed in a holdall he carried on the back of his bicycle. There was a satchel in front, and one of them folding things what they put their pictures on when they paints them."

"An easel?"

"That's it, sir."

"Anything else—an umbrella?"

"No, sir."

"Or a walking-stick?"

"No, sir."

"Are you quite sure? I want you to be very careful."

"I'm quite sure, Mr. Colson, and I'll tell you for why. First of all, I helped him undo his luggage when he arrived, and secondly, he borrowed this here stick—what used to belong to my late husband—several times when he went out walkin'. I can swear to that."

The detective glanced at a brown polished walking-stick with a knob at the end.

"All right," he said. "That's all I want to know. And I'll give you a bit of information in return. It's pretty certain *he* isn't the man we want."

"I'm glad to hear that, Mr. Colson. I liked the young feller."

The detective had turned to go, but paused a minute.

"It would be better for him still, Mrs. Yates, if you could prove that he was really in your house all night."

"Well, sir—I'm sure he was here till past one in the morning."

"Why?"

"He went to bed just before ten, sir. I had a toothache that night which kept me awake till just after one. And the way that young man snored was enough to keep anyone awake—let alone the toothache."

The detective laughed.

"That's all right, then."

"We've eliminated one of the three," he said to himself as he rode back. "And that's not a bad bit o' work, anyhow."

When he arrived at the police station the Canon was still there. The detective whispered a few words to the superintendent and Major Renshaw, and the latter said:

"You'll be glad to know, Canon, that we needn't detain this young man any longer. Would you like to see him before you go?"

"I should, very much."

When Grayson came in, Major Renshaw shook hands with him.

"We're quite satisfied about you, Mr. Grayson, and I must apologise for detaining you. But a stranger who goes off suddenly and mysteriously from the scene of a murder must expect to rouse suspicions—and you certainly did. Let me introduce you to my friend, Canon Fittleworth. You really owe your freedom this evening to him—though he won't tell you why, because he mustn't."

"I'm sure I'm most grateful to you, sir," said the young artist to the Canon.

"Delighted," replied the latter. "I'm so glad to have been of any use in getting you out of an awkward predicament."

"Now, Mr. Grayson," went on the Chief Constable, "we brought you in from Linderton this morning against your will. Will you allow me to send you back in my motor?"

"Well," replied Grayson, "I think I'll get a bed in Frattenbury. My holiday was nearly up, and I shall return to town to-morrow. I can walk out in the morning and get my machine and the rest of my belongings."

"No, you won't," said Major Renshaw, anxious to make amends. "I'll have them sent in—yes, you'll be comfortable at the 'Dolphin'— they shall be there early to-morrow morning. Good night—stop— let me have your address in case we want you."

The Canon, leaving his cigar box with the police, walked out of the station with Grayson and directed him to the hotel. Then he said:

"As the nearest relative of poor Templeton—I'm his cousin, you know—I should like to offer you a slight return for all the trouble you've gone through to-day. Will you give us the pleasure of dining with us to-night—at half-past seven?"

"It's awfully kind of you, sir—but I haven't any dress clothes with me."

"That doesn't matter in the least. You will? That's right, then. Good-bye for the present."

And the Canon chuckled as he went his way home. And his wife agreed he had done the right thing. When the Canon took the young artist into the drawing-room, just before dinner that night, Winnie Cotterill looked up with a start—and Grayson's eyes sparkled.

"Winnie!" he exclaimed, "I didn't expect to meet *you* here. This is a pleasant surprise."

"Miss Cotterill has been anxious to know about you," said Mrs. Fittleworth. "She heard you were in danger of arrest."

"So I brought you round to show her that you're really free," said the Canon, rubbing his hands.

"I'm most awfully glad to see—you've escaped from the police," said Winnie. "I *knew* you couldn't have done the murder."

"Come along," said the Canon. "Mr. Grayson, will you take my wife in to dinner, please?" and he offered his own arm to Winnie Cotterill.

"You're a perfect dear, Canon Fittleworth," said the girl as they crossed the hall. "How clever you must have been to get him off."

"Oh, *I* didn't get him off, as you call it, Miss Cotterill. I helped to explain something, that's all. Now you won't worry any more."

"Of course not."

"I don't think you need!" said the Canon dryly, a twinkle in his eye as he spoke.

CHAPTER XII.
Fresh Evidence

The three police officials, after the departure of the Canon and Grayson, looked thoughtfully at each other for a few moments. The Chief Constable said:

"Well—there's an end of young Grayson, as far as we are concerned."

Colson was heard to mutter something beneath his breath that sounded like "blighted parson." Then the Chief Constable went on:

"I've asked Canon Fittleworth, Colson, to try to remember anyone who had any of his cigars."

Colson nodded. He took one of the Canon's cigars out of the box, looked at it, put it in his case, and carefully examined the label on the outside of the box.

"Well?" asked the superintendent.

"I don't altogether depend on the Canon, sir. Other people might get hold of these cigars as well—if they've friends in Cuba, or are in the trade. Of course I agree with you, sir," he went on to Major Renshaw, "and we must take note of anyone who had a cigar from the Canon. But it isn't *there* I fancy that we shall find our man. May I venture to give an opinion?"

"Do," said the others.

"Well, it's fairly obvious that the original cigar band was changed while passing round the jury. I've got my suspicions—but I won't say just now."

"Ought we to tell the coroner, and get the jury—or any suspected person on it—dismissed?" asked Major Renshaw.

"By no means, sir. That's what I was just coming to. The man who changed that band should be the same as the individual who went after the walking-stick. We don't want to rouse his suspicions at this stage. Let him think the band has gone the same way as the stick—that we've lost both clues."

"How?" asked the superintendent.

"By making it public, just so far as we choose, and no farther. The blight—the Canon's bungled it up till now. If he'd only given us that band, instead of producing it at the inquest, we could have kept it dark. As it is, every newspaper's got a head-line with 'The Cigar Band Clue—What are the Police doing?' and all that rot. Well, let's keep it up. Let the public think we've tested the clue and that we're satisfied there's nothing in it."

"There's a lot in what he says," remarked the superintendent to the Chief Constable, who nodded agreement.

"Let the newspaper fellows know this—give 'em an 'official statement.' They love that. And if you, sir," to Major Renshaw, "could mention it, casual like, it would help."

"I'm dining out at Mr. Norwood's to-night," said the Chief Constable—"one of what he calls his bachelor dinners. Dr. Hazell is sure to be there. He's the biggest gossip in the place. It will be all over Frattenbury to-morrow if I mention it—ha, ha—'on the authority of the Chief Constable.'"

"That's exactly what I want, sir," said the detective eagerly. "It'll give more weight locally than all the newspapers. And I've got a sort of inspiration that we haven't to go out of the district to find our man."

"Unless, after all, it should happen to be Moss?" said the Chief Constable.

"He's not really out of the district—and we'll see him to-morrow," replied Colson.

"If there's nothing to keep us here, we're both going up to London to-morrow morning," explained the superintendent. "Oh, and by the way, sir, all known dealers in rough stones have been warned—and there's an eye being kept on certain fences. Not that it's likely that the murderer—if he's got the stones—would sell them just now."

"And it's probable that they're not far off," said Colson dryly.

"Well," said the Chief Constable, rising from his seat, "I'm off. I must dress for dinner. If you want me, Superintendent, ring up Norwood, he's on the phone. I shall be there till about eleven."

The little dinners which Francis Norwood gave periodically were as stiff and formal as Francis Norwood himself. But they were always good, and his port was of excellent vintage. There were four guests that night—all of the male sex. The coroner rarely invited ladies, and then only the wives of his intimate friends. He sat, stiff and erect, at the head of the table, on his right Major Renshaw and Sir Peter Birchnall, a local magnate and magistrate, on his left a clean-shaven, round-faced man of short but rather portly dimensions, who was the Dr. Hazell referred to by the Chief Constable, and a comfortable-looking clergyman, the Reverend Alfred Carringford, the vicar of the parish in which the coroner resided.

The maid—Norwood had no men-servants—had just put on the dessert with its accompaniments of wine and a box of cigars. Norwood passed round the port, and helped himself when it reached him again.

Sir Peter held his glass up to the light, took a sip, and smiled approvingly.

" '72, if 'm not mistaken, Norwood?"

Norwood nodded.

"Yes," he said. "I'm sorry to say I've only a few more bottles left. And it's too heavy a price to-day, even if there's any on the market."

Dr. Hazell raised his eyebrows and shook his head knowingly. Norwood was reputed to be a wealthy man, and the little doctor was sceptical.

"If you want to replenish your cellar, I can put you on to a good thing, Norwood," went on Sir Peter.

"Indeed?"

"Buy 'Virginian Reefs.' They're bound to go up. I happen to have seen the engineer's latest report. It's a safe thing."

" 'Virginian Reefs,' eh?" said Dr. Hazell, taking out his notebook. "You recommend them, do you, Sir Peter?"

"I hold some myself," replied the Baronet pompously, and with the air of one who could not be wrong.

Norwood shook his head and smiled his dry little smile.

"We lawyers are not over-keen on speculation," he said. " 'Virginian Reefs'—yes. I imagined they were in low water."

"Seven and sixpence was yesterday's price, but they'll go to three and four pounds. The general public know nothing yet, of course. This is the chance for picking them up."

Norwood, who was peeling an apple, at this point sent round the cigars. Carringford remarked as he lighted one:

"That was a strange circumstance—the discovery of that cigar band by Fittleworth in that Marsh Quay case."

He looked at Norwood as he spoke. The coroner replied stiffly:

"You can't expect me to discuss that, Vicar."

"I suppose not," said the doctor, "but it was a queer thing, as you say, Carringford. I suppose, Major," and he leaned his elbows on the table and looked across at the Chief Constable, "I suppose the whole thing is keeping you pretty busy?"

"Naturally," replied Major Renshaw, cutting and lighting his cigar.

"Now here," and the doctor held up the band he had just removed from his own cigar, "here is an innocent enough looking thing, and yet it might hang a man in this case, easily enough. You policemen have to note the merest trifles—well, just as we doctors do sometimes. A tiny symptom, Major—the flutter of an eyelid, a pain in the little finger, so to speak—but we know it points to a fatal disease. And I suppose you attach the greatest importance to this bit of red paper. It's *the* clue, isn't it?"

"Oh, come now," said Sir Peter, "you're asking leading questions of the police. It won't do, Doctor."

Major Renshaw removed the cigar from his mouth, puffed a volume of smoke across the table, and said: "Oh, I don't know. As a matter of fact, I don't mind saying that we attach very little importance to that cigar band."

"Really?" asked the coroner, sipping his port. "I confess I shouldn't have thought that—though I don't wish of course, to give an opinion."

"No," went on the Chief Constable, "I don't think there's much in it. And, as a matter of fact, we've tested it already. The brand was more common than Canon Fittleworth led us to suppose, and, after all, very likely had nothing to do with the murder at all. It might have been in the cabin for days."

"Dear me," said the doctor, who was listening intently. "That's rather a disappointment to you, isn't it?"

The Major shrugged his shoulders.

"It's not much use following up such a very doubtful clue," he admitted.

Norwood apparently did not care for the subject of the murder to be discussed. In his position as coroner this was natural. He addressed a counter-remark across the table to Carringford:

"I've just read the speech you made at the Diocesan Conference on Parochial Church Councils, Vicar. You must let me congratulate you."

The clergyman, pleased with the compliment, was launching forth on matters ecclesiastical—to the intense boredom of Sir Peter—when the maid entered.

"Please, sir, someone wants to speak to Major Renshaw on the telephone."

"You know where it is, Major—in the hall," said Norwood.

"Thanks."

The Chief Constable went to the telephone.

"Hullo—yes——"

The voice of the superintendent replied.

"Can you come at once, sir? It's important."

"All right."

"I'm sorry, Norwood," he said, as he went back into the dining-room, "but I'll have to go—I'm wanted."

"Anything fresh—about the murder?" asked Dr. Hazell.

"I don't know."

"Ah," said the doctor, pointing a finger at him, "you and I both get rung up in our professions. Only there's a difference. They call me up to save lives—and they summon you to help in catching an unfortunate wretch for the gallows, eh?"

"Perhaps. Good night," replied the Chief Constable.

When he reached the police station he found the superintendent, Colson, and a strong odour of stale beer, which emanated from the mouth of a peculiar individual. He was a rough-looking man of about forty, dressed in old, patched, corduroy breeches, brow leather gaiters, and a big, loose jacket, well-worn. He had a very red, beery-looking face, unbrushed black hair and whiskers, and a pair of sharp-looking dark eyes like a ferret's. The Chief Constable looked at him and said severely:

"It's you, is it, Thatcher? What mischief have you been up to now?"

The man shifted his dirty, soft hat from one hand to the other, and replied in a surly, thick tone of voice:

"I ain't done nothin', Major—s'elp me I ain't. I've told 'im what I come 'ere for."

And he jerked his head towards the superintendent.

"It's all right, sir," said that functionary, "he's come of his own accord this time. He wants to make a statement."

"What about?"

"That 'ere murder—over at Marsh Quay," said Thatcher.

"What do you know about it?"

"Look 'ere, Major," replied Joe Thatcher, "I doan't say as how I ain't got into trouble time and agen. *You* knows that. And I ain't given to have naught to do with the police as long as they lets me aloane—which they doan't always do, damn 'em! But I draws the line at murder, I does. I doan't hold with it, and that's why I come here to-night."

"Go on. What have you got to tell us?"

A wicked, artful leer broke over the man's face. "If I tells you what I knows—you woan't ask me what I was a-doin' of that night? I doan't want to come up before the beaks just because I was havin' a constitootional, as they calls it, when other folks were asleep."

"All right, Thatcher," said the superintendent. "We've got your record, and we know pretty well what you're up to when you take your midnight walks abroad. But you needn't fear in this case. If you've got any information about the murder at Marsh Quay we'll forget the rest."

"That's what my missus said, she did. I told her what I seen—and she says, 'You go and tell the police, Joe.' I kept on sayin' I wouldn't, and that's why I didn't come afore. An' she kept a-naggin' on me, till I saw life was going to be a little hell if I didn't come. And here I be."

"Go on, my man," said the Chief Constable encouragingly. "There's nothing to be afraid of; tell us about it."

"Well, 'tis like this. Saturday night I went out for a walk—late. I doan't say as I hadn't a gun wi' me—but that's naught to do wi' it—be it?"

"Nothing at all," said Major Renshaw with a laugh.

"I got down and round about them stubble-fields and spinneys along near the quay—but I didn't have no luck."

"No," said the Major dryly. "We had a big shoot there last week, and cleared out most of the birds."

"So I found," said the poacher brazenly. "Now—that 'ere wood, t'other side o' the water. Sometimes there's a goodish few—sparrers, we'll say—to be found there, and it wouldn't ha' been the first time as I'd borrowed one o' they canoes and slipped over for an hour or so. O' course I returned the canoe when I'd finished. I ain't no thief—thank Gawd!"

The others grinned at him, but were silent. It was best for the man to tell his story in his own way.

"It was between half-past twelve and one as I got down to the quay—I allus reckons to know the time within a few minutes—'tis a habit o' mine. There was no one about and 'twas a still night. There was a light on board that 'ere little yacht where the murder was, but I didn't hear any sound. I was a-standin' on the quay, a-makin' up my mind whether 'twas worth while crossing over, when I heard the sound of a boat bein' pulled across—from the other side."

"From the *other* side?" asked Colson.

"That's right. I wondered what anyone was a-doin' that time o' night—when respectable folk ought to be abed and asleep." He grinned. "I can see pretty well in the dark—I *has* to in my perfession—so I jist lay low and watched. Whoever it was, he warn't no boatman, by the way he mucked that 'ere boat about. The tide was flowin' in and he had to pull hard. When he got across he made straight for that 'ere yacht where the lights was burnin'. Clumsy, he was, too. He didn't 'arf bump the nose o' his boat into the yacht when he got to her. You could hear the bang all over the place."

"What did he do then?"

"Why, Major, he got aboard the yacht and went in the cabin. I see him quite plainly. But he never stayed there long. In less than five minutes he was out again, clamberin' into the boat, and pullin' away across stream as hard as ever he could go. Seemed in a mighty hurry, he did. Just then I heard the Cathedral clock strike one."

"What did you do?"

"I lit a pipe and waited a bit—quarter of an hour or less, I reckon. I was thinkin' it wouldn't do to cross over to the wood that night. And then the motor-car come along."

"The motor-car!" ejaculated the superintendent.

"Yes, sir—come down the road."

"To the quay?"

"No, sir. It stopped about thirty or forty yards before it got to the quay. I could see the lights."

"Did you see who was in it?"

"No, sir; I made tracks along the shore. Thinks I, 'There's too many folks about to-night for an honest chap to get a livin',' so I come straight home. And that's all about it."

They questioned him sharply, but he stuck to his story. Then the superintendent said:

"You'll probably have to tell all this to the jury—at the adjourned inquest."

"It won't get me into no trouble?" asked Thatcher.

"No," said the superintendent. "We'll see to that."

"Because," went on the man as he rose to go, "I've got my reputation to think of."

"We know all about that. And look here, Thatcher, keep your mouth shut," said the superintendent.

"How about the boats on the opposite shore?" asked the Chief Constable when Joe Thatcher had departed.

"There's only one," replied Colson, "belonging to Moss."

"Yes—to Moss," said the superintendent thoughtfully. "It looks ugly for him. We'll see this Isaac Moss to-morrow morning."

"I shall have to run down to Marsh Quay early before we start," remarked Colson.

"What for?"

"A little matter I want to look into. I wish this chap Thatcher had told us all this before."

"It doesn't matter much," said the superintendent. "It's just as well to have cleared off Grayson first. It leaves us a freer hand. I wish we knew more about that motor."

And the others agreed.

Early the following morning Colson was at Marsh Quay. He sought out Jim Webb, who was still in charge of the *Firefly*, sleeping aboard her, till he received instructions from her owner at Salcombe.

"Webb," he said, "I want you to row me over opposite."

"All right, sir."

"Pull to the yacht first. I want to see something."

He made Webb pull him all round the yacht till he found what he wanted.

"What do you make of this?" he asked, pointing to an indentation in her sides. The paint, especially the narrow green band, was badly rubbed, and the woodwork a little crushed. "Was this done before you came here?"

"No, sir. I'm sure it wasn't. I noticed it on Monday. Some of them reporter chaps—or someone—must have banged into her. They've been swarming about the place."

"Might have been caused by the nose of a boat running into her, eh?"

"That's exactly what I think, sir."

"All right, we'll go across now."

When they reached the farther shore he made for the small boat which was moored to the landing-stage, and examined her carefully. On her bows was a distinct smear of green paint.

"Humph," said the detective, "that seems to bear out Thatcher's story. That's the boat, sure enough. Webb," he went on, "wait here five minutes, will you? There's something I want to do."

"Yes, sir."

Colson disappeared along the pathway through the wood, carrying under his arm a long, thin brown-paper parcel he had brought. He began to unroll it as he went along.

In ten minutes or so he returned, the parcel under his arm, wrapped up once more. His brows knit and he was not looking best pleased. He hardly spoke to Jim Webb, and when he landed at once rode off on his bicycle.

"That's a frost," he muttered to himself; "at least, it looks like one. Anyhow, we'll see presently what Moss has got to say. He must be the man who crossed over to the yacht that night. It's pretty suspicious. But things don't altogether fit—though they *may* of course."

CHAPTER XIII.
Isaac Moss Explains

Standing on the platform of Frattenbury Station, waiting for the London train, were Harold Grayson and Winnie Cotterill. The superintendent, who was in plain clothes, raised his hat.

"Good morning, sir," he said with a smile. "I hope you won't think we are shadowing you up to town!"

"Oh, good morning, Superintendent. It certainly looks as if I hadn't quite escaped from your suspicions."

"Yes, you have, sir, I'm glad to say."

"Let me introduce you to Miss Cotterill. She is interested in this case."

The superintendent raised his hat again and bowed.

"I'm sorry, Miss Cotterill," he said, "if we've caused you any anxiety about Mr. Grayson."

She blushed a little as she replied:

"I confess it was a relief when Canon Fittleworth told us last night that Mr. Grayson was free."

An amused look lingered for a moment on the policeman's face as he glanced from one to the other.

"I'm more than ever pleased that our suspicions were unfounded," he said in a dry manner. "Here comes your train, sir. Are you both going up to London?"

"We are," said Grayson.

The police superintendent found an empty compartment and showed them in.

"Good morning," he said. Then he turned to Colson, who was standing near. "Come along, Colson. You and I won't disturb that young couple—and I hope nobody else will. We've both been in it ourselves, eh?"

There were other people in their compartment, so they maintained a rigid silence on the subject in hand. Colson was not sorry. He wanted to study the notes in his pocket-book and to think things out. Arrived in London, they took a taxi to Scotland Yard, and, after an interview with the authorities there, went on to Hatton Garden, where they found Tyler lounging about, also in plain clothes.

"Moss went into his office over an hour ago," he said. "You'll find him there."

The superintendent nodded and, followed by Colson, entered a block of offices and found his way to an upper floor. A door with ground glass panels bore the inscription "Mr. Isaac Moss." The superintendent opened it without knocking, and they found themselves in a little outer office. A girl, seated at a typewriter, rose hastily.

"Is Mr. Moss in?"

"He's particularly engaged, sir. He can't see anyone."

"Oh—indeed! But I must see him."

"I'm afraid you can't," said the girl. "He told me not to let anyone in—that I didn't know." The superintendent smiled at the girl's ingenuousness.

"Well," he said, "I'm afraid I must make you disobey orders. I'm a police superintendent." The girl paled a little, and went towards an inner door marked "Private."

"I'll tell him," she said.

But the superintendent was too quick for her. He was across the room in a moment.

"You must do what I tell you," he said. "Open the door. Don't be afraid."

As she opened the door a voice exclaimed:

"Who is it? I told you I couldn't see anyone."

"I'm afraid we must come in, all the same, Mr. Moss," said the superintendent, entering the room and followed by Colson.

A little dark man of evident Jewish persuasion, with a thin, black moustache, half rose from the chair in which he was seated. His face was deadly pale, his mouth was half open and his lips quivering.

"Who are you?" he asked, his voice shaking. "I don't know you."

"It's all right, Mr. Moss," broke in the superintendent closing the door, turning the lock and putting the key in his pocket. "I almost think you might have expected me to call. I'm Superintendent Norton, of the Frattenbury police"—he laid his card on the table—"and this is Detective-Sergeant Colson."

Then occurred a pitiable exhibition. Mr. Isaac Moss sank back in his chair, a cold sweat breaking out on his forehead, wringing his hands in a paroxysm of fright.

"I never murdered Mr. Templeton," he said. "I don't know anything about it. I wasn't there. I tell you it's no use you arresting me—I'm innocent. I never touched him. I knew you'd come. Oh," he moaned, "I knew you'd come, but I never murdered him, I tell you."

"Come, come, Mr. Moss," said the superintendent in a soothing tone, "I haven't made any charge against you yet. I warn you that the way you're going on will do you no good. Pull yourself together. I want to ask you some questions. Why, we detained a man yesterday who had every cause to be alarmed, with the facts there were against him, and he took it coolly enough."

"He's the man!" shrieked Moss. "He must be the man. You haven't let him go, have you? Why do you come to me? He's the man, I tell you."

Colson regarded the little writhing wretch with contempt mingled with pity. In his mind he was saying: "*He* hasn't got spunk enough to stab a fellow—even in his back."

The superintendent looked round the room.

"You don't happen to have any whisky—or brandy handy, do you?"

Isaac Moss sprang to his feet.

"Yes, I have," he cried. "You shall have a drink—of course you shall have a drink. You see it was the other man, don't you? Here——"

He had dashed to a cupboard and produced a bottle of whisky, a siphon and glasses. One of the latter fell to the floor with a crash. The superintendent poured out a stiff portion of the spirit, filled the glass up with soda-water and handed it to the terrified man.

"Drink it," he said. "Sit down now, and pull yourself together."

Moss gulped down the contents of the tumbler and sat looking at them. A slight colour came into his cheeks, but he was still trembling. The superintendent waited.

"What do you want?" asked Moss presently, in a slightly calmer tone of voice.

"Well, in the first place, bear in mind that I haven't arrested you. I want to ask you some questions."

As a matter of fact he had come determined to take Moss into custody. But he was accustomed to dealing with criminals, and had already half made up his mind that he need only detain him. And Moss had had fright enough as it was.

"Go on," said the Jew faintly.

"Well, then, will you tell us why you left your house near Marsh Quay so early and so suddenly on Sunday morning?"

"I didn't leave it suddenly," said Moss. "I had business in London—important business. I often come up on Sunday morning by that train."

"It won't do, Mr. Moss," said the superintendent, shaking his head. "We know you gave a sudden and unexpected order for your car early that morning. We know you are not in the habit of coming up to town on Sunday at all. For your own sake you'd better tell us the truth and hide nothing."

The little man wiped the sweat off his brow.

"Yes," he said, "I'll tell you the truth. I came away because I was frightened. So help me God, that's true."

"Frightened of what?"

"Lest I should be accused of being mixed up in Mr. Templeton's murder."

"How did you hear of his murder?"

"My man told me—early Sunday morning."

"It won't do, Mr. Moss," repeated the superintendent. "You had left the house before it was known that the murder had taken place. Come—if you can't tell me the truth, I shall have to take you away."

Isaac Moss wrung his hands.

"No—no!" he cried, "don't do that. My man didn't tell me. That was a lie. But I knew—I tell you I knew."

The superintendent looked at his notebook for a moment. Then he spoke.

"It would help us—and you, too—if you would tell us what you were doing on board Mr. Templeton's yacht at one o'clock on Sunday morning."

Moss started to his feet again.

"I wasn't there," he cried. "You're mistaken. I wasn't there."

"You *were* there," said the superintendent sternly. "I'll give you one more chance of speaking the truth, and if you don't I'll charge you with the murder of Reginald Templeton and take you into custody."

The wretched man sank into his chair again. Then he said, almost in a whisper:

"Very well, then—I was there."

"That's better," said the superintendent. "We'll go into that further in a moment. Now then," and he made a shot in the dark, "what have you done with the diamonds you took from Mr. Templeton?"

A little to the surprise of the two policemen the Jew, who was growing calmer under the influence of the stimulant, rose from his seat, unlocked a safe, took from it a small leather bag, very much like the one that had been found on the dead man, and poured its contents on the table.

"There they are," he said, "all but one—and that was the cause of the trouble."

"You stole these diamonds?"

"*Stole* them!" cried Moss. "*I* steal! Of course I never stole them. Ask anybody about me, and they'll tell you I'm a regular dealer in the stones. Besides—I gave Templeton the receipt for them. Didn't you find it? He put it in his pocket-book. I saw him do it."

The superintendent looked at Colson, who elevated his eyebrows, but said nothing. Both men were a little out of their reckoning. Then the superintendent said to Moss:

"See here, Mr. Moss. We police have a duty to do, but no innocent person need be afraid of us. We only want to secure the guilty. And we're always ready to help the innocent when we can. We know you were on Mr. Templeton's yacht—we know he had been with you on Saturday afternoon—and we know you left in the devil of a hurry and took these diamonds with you. You will serve your purpose, and ours, best by telling us all you know."

Isaac Moss took out his cigarette case.

"Do you mind if I smoke?"

"By all means."

He poured himself out some more whisky, drank it and said:

"Where do you want me to begin?"

"At the point when you had an interview with Templeton on Saturday afternoon. Tell us *why* he came to you."

"It was about these diamonds. I am agent for a firm in South Africa, Ehbrenstein & Co.—a well-known firm. They wrote telling me they had a consignment of uncut stones which they wished me to take to Amsterdam—to be cut, in the usual way of business. We are always very careful, of course, in these consignments, and if there is anyone well known to the firms or dealers coming over, it is a common thing to ask him to bring them. My letter of advice told me that Mr. Templeton—whom I knew slightly—would bring them over, and that I was to give him the receipt on delivery. It would, of course, be a matter of commission for him. The letter also said that he would communicate with me when he reached England. He didn't at first. I knew the boat on which he was sailing had arrived in Plymouth, and grew anxious, especially as I knew that Templeton was an erratic and peculiar man, with little regard for business methods. Then I heard from him—from Poole—saying he was yachting on the South Coast, probably finishing up at a little place called Marsh Quay, when he would run up to town and deliver the stones. He also told me to write to him at the G.P.O., Ryde, if I had anything to say. I was getting still more anxious, and wrote at once, suggesting that as, by a coincidence, I had a week-end place at Marsh Quay, he should bring me the stones there. I described exactly where my house stood. He replied saying he would be with me on Saturday afternoon."

"Yes, we know that," said the superintendent.

"I was sitting on my lawn when he came. We talked a bit there, and then went into the house—into my study, and had a whisky and soda each. It was there that he produced these stones—in a little bag like this one—and I turned them out on the table and counted them. There were thirty-two—the correct number. I put them back in the bag and gave him the receipt. Just before he went he said, 'I'd like to keep that little bag. I've carried it a good many hundred miles.' I said, 'Certainly.' I unlocked a drawer in my writing-desk, emptied the stones into a little tin box, locked it up and gave him the bag. Then I walked down to my landing-stage and watched him row back to his yacht. That was the last I saw of him—alive."

He drank a sip or two out of his glass; he was beginning to get agitated again.

"Take your time," said the superintendent. "Tell us everything, mind."

"Yes, I will. When my wife and I went to bed that night it was late—after twelve. I took the little box containing the stones with me—I have a small safe in our bedroom. Before I put them away the thought struck me that I would count them. To my horror, there were only thirty-one—one of the largest was missing. You must remember that these stones are worth a considerable sum, and I only hold them as agent—but I am responsible for them. My wife and I talked it over, and came to the conclusion that I must have left one stone in the bag when I emptied them out the second time. I was in a dilemma. For all I knew, Templeton might be off with the tide very early the next morning—he hadn't told me his movements. Then I looked out of the window—you can see across the estuary over the trees. I could make out a light. Now, I know the position of the lights there, and I knew at once it couldn't be the inn or the house in which—what's his name?—the old retired cigar merchant lives. Yes?"

Colson had sprung to an upright position on his chair.

"What's that you say?" he asked. "A cigar merchant? Who?"

"Why—he lived in the house opposite the 'Mariner's Arms'—ah—Proctor's his name. Didn't you know?"

"Was he in the cigar trade?"

"Yes—till about two years ago. I knew him slightly up here; in fact, it was I who told him about that house of his being for sale."

Colson gave a low whistle and exchanged glances with the superintendent.

"Sorry I interrupted. Go on, Mr. Moss."

"Well, from the position of the light, I guessed it must be on Templeton's yacht, and that he had not yet turned in. I didn't know, as I told you, whether he might not be off—even soon, for the tide would be on the turn between one and two. And I hadn't the slightest idea how to get hold of him if he left, so I said to my wife, 'I'll get that stone now. Templeton's evidently on his yacht.' 'How?' she asked. 'Why,' I replied, 'it's quite simple; it's only a question of pulling over in the boat.' At first she was rather inclined to dissuade me, but she saw how anxious I was to get the stone back, so at last she said, 'Well, hurry up, then, Isaac, and get it over. I want to go to sleep—and don't stop gossiping with Mr. Templeton.'"

"And you went?" put in the superintendent.

Moss nodded, took a drink and went on.

"I did. It wasn't so easy as I thought. The tide was running in hard, and I'm not much of a hand with a boat. I had to pull with all my might, and when I got to the calmer water, where the yacht lay, I still pulled so hard that I ran into her with a bit of a bump. I was rather surprised that no one took any notice; it must have shaken her."

"Well, I fastened my boat to the yacht and got aboard. There wasn't a sound. The cabin door was open, and I went in. The hanging lamp was burning. I looked round, and there I saw Templeton lying on the floor—face downwards. At first I thought he was asleep, or drunk. Then I stooped down. Ah, my God—it's haunted me ever since!"

He leaned forward for a moment and covered his face with his hands. Then he went on.

"There was a pool of blood on the floor; he was dead."

"Yes—and then?" asked the superintendent.

"I—I—thought I should have fainted. I sat down on one of the bunks for a minute. Then the horror of the thing took hold of me. If I were discovered—what would be the position? It flashed across me instantly—that dark night—no one else about—I saw it all. They would think *I* did it.

"I got out of that cabin in a panic and into my boat. I don't know how I managed to get across—it seemed hours—and I pulled till my arms ached with pain. As soon as I reached my house I ran upstairs and told my wife what had happened. She was as frightened as myself—she saw the danger. We neither of us got a wink of sleep that night. We kept talking it over, and at last we both agreed that the wisest thing to do would be to get away very early in the morning—we hoped before the discovery was made."

"The worst thing you could have done," interposed Colson. "It naturally drew suspicion upon you at once. We knew Templeton had been with you in the afternoon, and one of the first things we did was to try to get hold of you—and found you'd bolted."

"I know—I know," said Moss. "I've been in terror ever since. I've sat in this office, trying to do business, and expecting every moment to see the police come in—it's been agony."

"What you ought to have done," said the superintendent, "was to give the alarm—at Marsh Quay—directly you discovered the body."

"Yes—yes—but even suppose I had—wouldn't you have suspected me? I don't know. I don't know."

The superintendent did not answer. He was thinking what *he* would have done, if he had been a nervous, cowardly man in a like predicament. And he had to agree, mentally, that the Jew had acted according to his natural temperament.

"That's the whole truth, so help me God!" said Moss earnestly, "and I'm glad I've told you now; it's a blessed relief. I couldn't have gone on much longer. What are you going to do with me?" he asked, throwing out his hands in appealing gesture.

The superintendent did not reply for a moment. He was considering. Then Colson whispered something to him, and he nodded.

"Sergeant Colson wants to ask you a question—before we decide anything."

"Yes?" said the Jew.

"I may as well tell you," said Colson, "that you have been under strict observation for the last few days. But there's one thing I want to know. When you and your wife came up to London on Sunday morning, apparently you did not go to your house in Brondesbury. We've ascertained that you only went there on Monday. Where were you on Sunday night? If you can tell us that, and bring witnesses to prove the truth of it, it will materially help you."

He was, of course, thinking of the incident of the walking-stick. Already he was more than half satisfied with the Jew's story—it fitted in with his own deductions. But he wanted to make quite sure. For this would help him still more.

"No—we didn't go home," said Moss, "we were not expected—our two maids at Brondesbury had the week-end off. We went to an hotel and stayed the Sunday night there."

"What hotel?"

"The 'Chester.' "

"Will you come with us to the 'Chester' now?" asked the superintendent. "We should like to corroborate this statement."

"Certainly—I will come."

"Go down and get a taxi," said the superintendent to Colson, "and ask Tyler to come with us."

The Jew was putting on his overcoat as Colson left the room; he turned a nervous, inquiring glance on the superintendent.

"Tyler is one of our men," said the latter dryly. "He's been shadowing you since Monday. I hope," he added, in a more kindly tone, "to take him back with us to Frattenbury."

Arrived at the "Chester," the superintendent produced his card and asked to see the manager. A few minutes later they were closeted with him in his private office.

"I want you to tell us," said the superintendent, "whether this gentleman," and he indicated Moss, "stayed here on Sunday night last."

"The name?"

"Moss—Isaac Moss."

"Certainly. Wait here a moment, and I'll make inquiries."

"I should like to have everything corroborated."

"All right."

The manager returned after a brief interval, bringing with him the booking clerk, the hall porter and a chambermaid. The booking clerk at once recognised Moss, produced his registration signature, and the entry in the book. The chambermaid stated that he and his wife had occupied room number 87.

"Can any of you swear—I warn you that it may have to come to that—that Mr. Moss was in the hotel all Sunday night?"

"Up to twelve o'clock would be enough," broke in Colson.

"I can do that," said the hall porter; "at least I know he was here from nine p.m. till midnight. He sat in the lounge most of the time. I saw him writing a letter, which he gave me to post just before he went to bed—a minute or two after twelve. I saw him get into the lift, and said good night to him. I'm quite prepared to swear to this."

"Very well," said the superintendent, "that's all I want to know. Can we be alone—my friends and I—for a minute or two?" he asked the manager.

"Certainly. Make use of this room. Nothing wrong, I hope, superintendent?"

"No—it's all right."

When the manager and the others had gone, the superintendent said:

"Well, Mr. Moss, I've decided not to take you into custody, though I may as well tell you now that I quite intended to do so. You've been exceedingly imprudent, and you've had a narrow escape. As to these diamonds"—he had put them back in the bag and pocketed them—"can you satisfy me that you have a right to them?"

"I have all the correspondence relating to them in my office—and I can bring another proof. Ehbrenstein & Co. sent full particulars of the transaction to another of their London agents—this is frequently done, as a covering precaution."

"Very good, we will return to your office and see this agent. If it is as you say, I am prepared to leave the stones with you."

"How about—how about the other stone—you found it on Mr. Templeton, I hope?"

The man's Jewish instincts were predominating now that the crisis was over.

"You'll get that—in good time. Now, Mr. Moss, I don't want to have any further trouble with you. If all is as you say, and I allow you your freedom, you must be prepared to tell your story to the jury at the remanded inquest. You understand?"

"Do you think," hesitated Moss, a little of his terror returning, "that they'd be likely to return a verdict of—of—murder against me?"

"It doesn't matter in the least what they do," said the policeman with fine sarcasm in his opinion of the brain powers of the "twelve good men and true." "It's only a coroner's jury. We might have, in that case, for form's sake, to bring you before the magistrates' court. But you'd never get committed for trial. *We'll* see to that."

The end of it was that the superintendent expressed himself satisfied, released Isaac Moss, and returned to Frattenbury with Colson. In the course of the journey the detective remarked:

"I never expected we should find Moss to be our man. When I showed his housekeeper and her husband that stick this morning, pretending I had found it in their master's boat, and they both denied that they had ever seen it before, I felt pretty certain. Besides, I thought beforehand that the stick was too long to be used by a little man like Moss. Well, that settles *his* book," and he rubbed his hands. "We've eliminated *two* out of the three. Now we'll go for the last one. A cigar merchant, eh, sir? That's a bit significant."

The superintendent nodded.

"What are you going to do, Colson?"

"Leave that to me for a bit, sir. I've got a card up my sleeve that ought to take the trick. And I'll play it—before the adjourned inquest!"

Smoking his pipe that evening, in his snug little home, he related the events of the day to his wife.

"And now for Mr. Joseph Proctor, retired cigar merchant!" he exclaimed gleefully.

She took his hand as she sat beside him.

"Be careful dear!" she said.

"Why?"

"You've just told me that Mr. Moss is a little man, and would scarcely have carried a long walking-stick."

"Well?"

"Isn't Mr. Proctor a little man, too?"

"Confound it!" he exclaimed.

Then his face lightened. "It's all right," he said. "If he bought the stick in Switzerland he'd have to take what they'd got. And he wouldn't use it in the ordinary way there—in climbing with it. Besides——"

"Besides what?"

"There's more ways than one of carrying a walking-stick, my dear. I've observed that. Little men often simply *carry* them—I mean, they don't hold them by the handle and stick the point in the ground when they walk."

She squeezed his hand fondly.

"You are a silly old dear," she said with a laugh. "That reasoning might have applied to Mr. Moss, you know."

"One for you," he replied. "Never mind, old girl, Moss is out of the game now."

CHAPTER XIV.
Reginald Templeton's Letter

Anthony Crosby looked up with a smile as Winnie Cotterill was ushered into his private office.

"Good morning, Miss Cotterill. Very glad to see you," he said, getting up from his chair and shaking hands with the girl. "You got my note, then?"

"You said you wanted to see me, Mr. Crosby."

"I did. Sit down, won't you? Now I dare say you've been wondering why I've enticed you into my office, eh?"

"Is it anything about Mr. Templeton's murder?" asked Winnie as she sat down.

"Well—er—in a way it is."

"Have the police found out yet who did it?" asked the girl eagerly.

The lawyer took up some typewritten sheets lying on his table and glanced at them.

"The superintendent at Frattenbury has been good enough to send me a private report," he replied. "I don't think I'm betraying their confidence when I tell you that so far they haven't laid their hands on the villain. There was another man they suspected—besides Mr. Grayson—but he seems to have cleared himself."

Winnie had taken off her gloves. The observant lawyer glanced at her left hand.

"You're very glad Mr. Grayson is no longer suspected?" he asked dryly.

The girl blushed a little, smiled and nodded.

"Yes," she said. "You see—since I saw you last——"

"You've added to your jewellery, eh, Miss Cotterill?"

"Mr. Grayson asked me to marry him, and I said——"

" 'Yes.' I'm not surprised. Let me offer you my congratulations. When are you going to be married?"

"Oh, it'll be ever so long a time. You see, Harold's got to make his way as an artist. He's the youngest son. He's getting on, of course. But we shall have to wait a bit."

"And you—do you manage to earn your own living?"

"Oh, yes—just, you know. I haven't been able to save anything. But I'm getting along nicely."

"I see. Well, Miss Cotterill, we'll dismiss this naturally pleasant subject for a time, if you don't mind. I'll tell you why I asked you to call. I suppose you know that my late client was much interested in you?"

"Uncle?—Mr. Templeton? He was most awfully good to me."

"I wonder if you know why?" said the lawyer.

"Sometimes I've often tried to guess—I've wondered if he was fond of my mother, you know?"

Crosby nodded. "Yes—he was, Miss Cotterill. He was in love with her before she married."

A deep blush spread over the girl's face.

"You haven't sent for me to tell me he—he was my fa——"

"No, no, no, my dear young lady. I assure you. Besides, you probably remember your father?"

And he looked at her keenly.

"Yes—very faintly. You see, I was very young when he died—I couldn't have been more than four years old. I can just remember him—not what he was like, you know. That's all. I asked because—because my mother hardly ever mentioned him—she didn't seem to care to talk about him—and I wondered——"

"Yes, yes," interposed the lawyer sympathetically. "I understand. Well, you can dismiss any such thought from your mind."

"Can you tell me anything about my father?"

He looked at her a moment, and then said:

"No, I can't tell you anything about him. But I can tell you something that ought to please you," he went on with a smile. "Mr. Templeton made his will, and left it with me before he went to South Africa. Here it is," and he held up a paper. "Can you guess the contents?"

"How can I, Mr. Crosby?"

"Well, he's left everything of which he died possessed to you!"

"To *me!*" she exclaimed, in astonishment. "Oh, no—there must be some mistake."

He laughed.

"It's very rude of you to doubt a lawyer's word, my dear young lady. And you ought not to be surprised. His only relations, apparently, were the Fittleworths, and they're quite well off. Now, don't jump to conclusions. You're not going to be an heiress by any means, so don't you think it. Mr. Templeton wasn't at all rich, and he spent most of his money in travelling and fitting out expeditions. I've been looking over his affairs, and you'll only get two thousand pounds at the outside."

"Two thousand pounds!" cried Winnie. "I never expected to have so much money in all my life. Do you really mean it?"

"I wish everyone was as modest in their ideas of money as you are. No I don't, though—I should have to lower my fees! Yes, it's about two thousand, as far as I can make out. Now, what are you going to do with it?"

He leaned back in his chair and smiled at her. Visions of gowns, hats, jewellery, furniture, and finally a trousseau flitted through the girl's mind. And the lawyer, who had a knowledge of human nature—intensified by being a married man—shrewdly guessed several of the visions.

"I—don't—know," said Winnie slowly. "There are ever so many things, and——"

"Now look here, Miss Cotterill," broke in Crosby, "may I presume to give you a bit of advice? If you invest the money carefully, it ought to bring you in a hundred a year."

He knew what the answer would be. And it was.

"Oh, Mr. Crosby, can't I have *some* of it to spend now?"

"You can have the whole lot if you like—when we've taken out probate. It's yours absolutely."

"I shouldn't want to spend it *all*. I shouldn't know how to."

"Oh, I expect you would. Anyhow—I don't want to force myself on you—but will you let me arrange matters? Suppose you have a hundred pounds and let me invest the remainder for you, eh?"

Her eyes sparkled.

"That would be just ripping!" she said. "Thank you ever so much."

"Very well. I'll see about taking out probate, and let you know when I shall want you again."

He had adopted his professional manner and looked at his watch markedly.

"There isn't anything else just now. Good-bye, Miss Cotterill; and hearty congratulations—in a double sense."

When Winnie Cotterill had departed, the lawyer took up another paper that was lying on his desk, and read it carefully. The sealed packet he had mentioned to Canon Fittleworth had contained it. It was in the form of a letter from Reginald Templeton.

My Dear Crosby,

We are all of us in the lap of the gods, and sometimes they drop us before we think they will. Anyhow, when a man starts, as I am starting, for some considerable time abroad, one never knows what may happen. So this is for your private eye in case I cut the traces or they are cut for me—and don't see you again.

You have my will, in which I leave the little I've got to Winnie Cotterill—and I expect you know the reason. But there's something else I want to tell you about the girl, which I think you ought to know in case the unforeseen may happen—as it does sometimes. Her name isn't really Cotterill at all—it's Forbes. Don't start, my friend, there's nothing wrong with her parentage. The facts are these. Her mother, Mabel Cotterill, didn't marry me as I hoped she would. She chose a man named Percy Forbes, a young lawyer. He turned out a wrong 'un. When Winifred was about four years old, he was tried on a serious charge of embezzlement, and sentenced to seven years' penal servitude. He hadn't got a leg to stand upon, it was a clear case. He and his wife were living at the time—well, it doesn't matter where. But Mrs. Forbes naturally left the neighbourhood; in fact I advised her to do so. The question arose about Winifred. The mother didn't want the child to hear of the family disgrace, so she went to a neighbourhood where nobody knew her, and took her maiden name of Cotterill. We used to talk over matters sometimes—as to what would happen when Forbes came out of prison—and she hated the thought of the child ever knowing that her father had been a convict. But Forbes didn't come out of prison—he died at Princetown in the third year of his sentence. So Winifred was brought up to believe that he died when she was four years old—and that's all she knows. And her mother stuck to the name of Cotterill.

What do I want you to do? Probably nothing, my friend. I trust you to keep up the fiction. A name doesn't matter, and the girl will, I hope, marry some good fellow, and so get another name that she's a right to. You will agree that it is best not to let her have the burden of her father's disgrace.

But—and this is the real object of this letter—if ever there's a question of her benefiting by the knowledge (I don't suppose there ever will be), I wanted you to know the facts. It seemed to me to be only fair to her. And, in that case, I ask you to use your own discretion—just as I should have done. You're a wiser man than I am but even I could solve the problem as to whether it would be better for the girl to know of her father's crime for the sake of any material advantage that might occur, or whether a mind based on the contentment of ignorance is not really worth more than worldly dross.

I know I'm a queer chap, and it's because I'm queer that I haven't mentioned places. You're shrewd enough to find out the facts for yourself if occasion arises. And as the finding out of the facts would take you a little time, I've tied you up, so that you can have plenty of leisure for decision.

That's all. If the aforementioned gods drop me, you'll see that Winifred gets my little lot of possessions. And to recompense you for this—and for making further investigations if you have to do so—please take the enclosed bank-note for a hundred pounds, with every good wish from

- Your sincere friend,
- Reginald Templeton.

The lawyer carefully replaced this document in its envelope and locked it up.

"A queer letter," he said to himself; "but then, Templeton was not an ordinary sort of man. Of course, I can easily find out about this fellow Forbes, if I want to, but it seems to me, at present, that there's nothing to do—yes, it wouldn't be fair to tell the girl. I can quite understand the policy of bringing her up in ignorance of her father's crime.

"Well, anyway," he went on, "this matter has nothing to do with the murder."

He took up the superintendent's letter and read it again.

"So Moss is out of the running," he soliloquised, "and the diamonds are accounted for. So it could hardly be robbery—unless," and he went on thoughtfully, "unless, of course, someone else knew he had those diamonds on him—and did not know he had handed them over to Moss. That looks feasible. It's a rational motive for the crime. I wonder who this other suspect is that the police say they have an eye on?

"There's another queer thing about this murder," he reflected. "Hardly any papers were found in the cabin, and none on Templeton's body. Yet there were about thirty pounds in notes in the open locker. If the murderer was after the diamonds, and didn't find them, why did he take any papers? For Templeton must have had a pocket-book or something on him. It's a rum case. I wonder if the police will ever solve it. Well, perhaps there will be some fresh light at the inquest. Anyhow, I can't give any more time to it just now."

It wasn't long before Winnie Cotterill saw Grayson. He called at the flat and had tea. Maude Wingrave came in just after he had arrived.

Winnie told them the news.

"Poor Uncle!" she said; "I'd rather not have had the money when it means his death, of course. But I just can't help being excited. Look here, you children! You've both got to dine with me to-night—at the 'Petit Cygne.' I'll stand treat."

"Squanderer!" derided Maude. "Beware, Mr. Grayson! She'll throw your money about like ducks and drakes. I don't think I'll come, Winnie."

"Why not, old thing?"

"You two irresponsible young persons having entered upon the broad downward path that leadeth into the narrow straights of matrimony with insufficient income will do all the talking to one another—and it will be appalling to listen unto. That's why."

"I'll promise to address quite a lot of remarks to you," said Grayson.

"Yes, I know—'Don't you think Winnie looks charming to-night?' and all that sort of unbearable——"

"Shut up, Maude—don't be rude. Please excuse her, Harold. I'm trying to teach her manners—she spent the extra tuppence on frivolity. You'll both come, and there's an end of it."

"The end of it will be that I shall leave you two children at the close of the meal, see?"

"*We* don't mind, do we, Harold?"

"Not a bit," replied Grayson, as if he meant it.

"You're not polite, Mr. Grayson," said Maude. "If you don't treat me with due respect, I shall stay till the bitter end."

But, being a good-hearted girl, of course she didn't.

CHAPTER XV.
Detective-Sergeant Colson's Deductions

The newspaper paragraphs about the murder at Marsh Quay dwindled in length. There were several scathing leading articles dealing with the inefficiency of the local police, and expounding the systems that ought to be put into force. One leader-writer produced an article conclusively proving that the Government was to blame. Writers of that peculiar terse and asterisked matter—the editor, it is presumed, puts in the asterisks in exchange for the copy he deletes—which adorns the "magazine" page of certain of our morning papers reaped a small crop of guineas. Thus one of them described the manufacture of cigar bands another epitomised half a dozen yacht tragedies, and a third gave a graphic sketch of how he himself had sailed in the Marsh Quay estuary.

The Sunday papers, of course, had their contributions. "An Expert in Crime" brilliantly reconstructed the whole murder, hinted at clues which the police ought to have found, and, without mentioning any names, left the impression on the mind of the reader that the two sailor-men, to wit, Jim Webb and Tom Gale, had acted in collusion, with the assistance of Mrs. Yates, who had countenanced a mysterious rendezvous at the "Mariner's Arms."

The police were inundated with letters—suggestive and critical. People called at the police station to make statements, which were patiently received and laid on one side. But, as usual, the police quietly kept their own counsel and were unimpressed.

Colson, who was now in the best of spirits, called on Canon Fittleworth.

"I'm sorry," said the Canon, "but my list isn't quite complete yet. I shall have to make a few more efforts of memory, as Major Renshaw puts it. I'm not satisfied."

"What list, sir?"

"Why, the names of all the people I can remember who smoked any of my cigars."

"Oh, *that*!" exclaimed the detective. "Yes, I know. But it wasn't about that list that I called—later on will do very well. I came to ask you for the name and address of your friend in Cuba who sent you the cigars."

"My Spanish friend. Certainly. I'll write it down for you. What do you want it for?" he asked, as he passed it over to Colson.

"Oh—it may be useful," said the detective in a non-committal manner. "One never knows."

"Any further progress?"

The Canon, of course, was interested.

"You mustn't ask me, please, sir. We're doing all we can."

Later on that day the police sent a cablegram to Cuba, asking for certain information. Also, Colson ran up to London, and was closeted for some time with the managing director of a reputable firm of wholesale cigar importers, from whom he gathered certain details which he carefully entered in his notebook.

"They're first-rate cigars, aren't they?" asked the managing director at the close of the interview. "Of course, there are very few of them manufactured. We keep them to ourselves."

"I don't know anything about them in that way," replied the detective dryly. "I haven't smoked one."

"Haven't you? Well, you shall then. I've got some of them here. Take half a dozen. Anything else I can do for you, let me know. So you know Proctor, eh? Nice little chap. Asked me to run down and see him some day."

"I'd rather you said nothing about my visit, if you do, sir. You will understand I've been asking you for this information in confidence."

"Quite. I won't say a word. Not that I'm likely to see him yet awhile."

The detective agreed that the brand was an excellent one as he smoked one of the cigars on his return journey. He also read, in the evening paper, one of the aforenamed articles on the lethargy of the provincial police—and enjoyed it immensely. But, then, he was in the mood for enjoying anything just then.

"By the way, Colson," said the superintendent to him when they were in consultation that evening, "have you made any more progress with that blotting-paper puzzle, 'Ezra's ices'?"

"Not much, sir. I think I've found out two or three more words. But I don't attach importance to it. We've something more definite than that to go upon."

"True—but I'd bear it in mind all the same. We mustn't neglect any detail."

"All right, sir. I'm feeling a little bit off colour," he went on, with a grin. "I think a little fresh air will do me good. So I propose taking a day's holiday to-morrow and spending it at Marsh Quay. I may even stay the night, sir."

"Very well, Colson," replied the superintendent, grinning at him in return. "I hope it will set you up. Don't get into mischief."

"I may commit a burglary, sir—that's all. It's a fascinating game when you're on a holiday. If possible—if I get any luck, that is—it won't come off. But I'll come back and give myself up to you if it does."

Colson seemed about to carry out his threat next day by taking with him a jimmy, a strong pocket-knife, and a bunch of skeleton keys—carefully selected from trophies at the police station.

The house in which Proctor resided at Marsh Quay was exactly opposite the spot where the yacht had been anchored. The main entrance was from the road, just before the quay was reached. A low stone wall, running parallel with the estuary, bordered the garden on the western side, and a small gate led through this wall to the shore; in fact Proctor had come out of this gate when he had accosted Jim Webb and Mrs. Yates on the morning when the murder was discovered.

The *Firefly* was no longer riding in the little harbour. Acting on the instructions of her owner, Jim Webb by this time was sailing her back to Salcombe. Local interest in the scene of the murder had subsided, and the detective had the place practically to himself.

He had found out all that he could about Mr. Proctor's household and habits. That was not very difficult. The unsuspecting landlady of the "Mariner's Arms," in the course of an apparently casual conversation, had told him that the boy Philip had left, and that his great-uncle was once more by himself. He also gathered that Proctor's domestic establishment consisted of an elderly cook-housekeeper and a young maidservant, both of whom slept at the back of the house, while Proctor himself occupied a bedroom over the dining-room with a view, south and west, of the estuary.

He further ascertained that it was the little man's usual habit, when alone, to walk into Frattenbury in the afternoon, where he read the papers at a club.

It was the afternoon now, and he had seen Proctor start towards Frattenbury across the field path, so he felt free and unobserved. There were several things that he wanted to do. First of all he wanted to saturate his mind with a mental vision of the committal of the crime. It was not the first time, of course, that he had taken a careful survey, but he wished to reconstruct the scene, as he had imagined it, more closely.

For this purpose he took up a position on the shore just by the little garden gate. Then he soliloquised:

"Yes—now suppose anyone in the house, or garden, were on the lookout for Templeton's return—Wait a bit, though. Something might have happened before then. It was, probably, only the thought of robbery in the first place.

"By Jove!" he exclaimed presently, "I believe I've got it—it would account for the stick in the dinghy and everything else. This way.

"Let us call the murderer A. Well, A has reason to believe that Templeton has those diamonds, and he doesn't know that he has already given them to Moss. He has seen Jim Webb go off to Frattenbury—probably found out that he was staying the night there. And he has seen Templeton go, too. He could easily find out if he was expected back late or not. Tom Gale knew it, Grayson knew it, Jim Webb knew it—they talked it over in the inn. And Mrs. Yates knew it—she told me she'd remarked about it to others.

"Well, then, A, with this information, speculates that Templeton might leave the diamonds on board. Quite likely. It was a dark night and a lonely walk. He determines to take a chance on this. But he can't do it till the coast is quite clear. That wouldn't be till after closing time—ten o'clock. He waits about outside, probably in the garden, taking his stick with him. He may have armed himself with a knife—ah! that's it, he took a tool of some sort—very likely an old dagger, as the doctor pointed out, to prise open any locks. Capital!

"What next? As he stood there waiting, he lighted a cigar—being an inveterate smoker—from force of habit. He would hear the men come out of the inn at ten o'clock; he would hear Tom Gale walk off along the quay, and then all would be quiet, with a clear coast.

"He goes down to the shore now. The dinghy is afloat. It's much more simple to use her for his purpose than to run a canoe down to the water—and less noisy. He gets into the dinghy, laying his walking-stick down in the stern—a natural action, because the seat for the rower is well aft—pulls out to the yacht, gets on board and makes the dinghy fast.

"Then he lights the lamp. That's all right, because anyone seeing it would naturally conclude the owner is aboard. People knew he was sleeping there that night. And he begins to make his search.

"But Templeton comes back sooner than A expected. A man doesn't generally leave a house where he's dining so early. But we know Templeton did. He sees the light on board, finds the dinghy has gone, and wonders what is up. Possibly he jumps to the conclusion that Jim Webb has come back after all. A canoe is lying there handy; he runs her down to the water and paddles aboard.

"Meanwhile A, still smoking his cigar from force of habit, has burnt it down to the band; he flicks it off, or it drops off by itself. Then he hears Templeton coming aboard. He is caught in the act.

"He has the tool or dagger, whatever it is, in his hand. Possibly his first impulse is to hide—behind the table. But Templeton comes into the cabin, and, for the moment, hesitates in astonishment. The folding table is between them—that prevents a struggle. And then the climax comes. A, either desperate at being discovered or acting on a murderous instinct for the sake of the jewels—he hadn't found them, and both lockers were open, as we know—probably the former, reaches over the table and aims a blow at the unlucky Templeton—a blow which proves fatal.

"Then he probably pauses to think—he may even take a look outside, or listen to hear if anyone is about. He knows he's risked his neck for the sake of those diamonds. He's a cool hand and calculates there's no *greater* risk—now the deed is done. So he takes out of Templeton's pockets his wallet—anything he can find—he isn't going to examine them at the moment—he knows he must clear out as quickly as possible. He puts his hand under the body and feels the waistcoat pockets—they are quite flat, so he doesn't bother about them, little knowing that he misses the only stone there is.

"His next move is to get back. Not the dinghy—the canoe, of course. The dinghy might arouse suspicion if found on the shore in the morning with the canoe fast to the yacht. In his haste and trepidation, he forgets the stick he has left in the dinghy till afterwards. Probably he is indoors by this time. He daren't return that night. It's too big a risk. And he daren't remove the stick the next day; people are about from the beginning. His only chance to recover that stick is to do exactly what he did do—on Sunday night. There! What do you think of that?"

He addressed the remark out loud to a solemn-looking rook that had perched for a moment on a post opposite to him.

And the rook flapped its wings and replied:

"Caw! Caw!"

And then flew away as if it was not a bit impressed—which it ought to have been. For Detective-Sergeant Colson's reasoning was so very clear and lucid that he felt it was going to hang a man and give him promotion.

Colson, unabashed, by the irresponsive and somewhat impertinent rook, went on with his construction methods.

"When A had examined the contents of Templeton's pockets," and he chuckled, "he was a little disappointed, I fear. Of course, he burnt the lot. We shall never find them, but we *shall* find A!"

Having arrived at this conclusion, to his great satisfaction, Colson turned his thoughts to the other object for which he had visited Marsh Quay that day. He wanted to get, somehow, into Proctor's house, and that without anyone knowing about it. He was quite prepared, if occasion brought the necessity, to make a burglarious entry that night, for which purpose he was minded to reconnoitre and view possible means of entrance. There was another method of course. He could ring the front-door bell, boldly ask to see Proctor, and, finding that he was out, beg to be allowed to remain until he returned. The only hindrance to this procedure was that he would arouse Proctor's suspicions, which he was not anxious to do. There was a third way out of it, but rather risky. If he could satisfy himself that the two domestics were out of hearing in the kitchen at the back of the house, he might be able to slip in now—and try to find out what he wanted to know.

The way in which he really did enter the house was entirely unforeseen by him. He went into the garden, through the little green gate, and was beginning carefully to observe how the windows of the dining-room opened, when, out of the front door, cigar in mouth, walked Mr. Proctor himself. Afterwards he ascertained that Proctor had, after walking half-way to Frattenbury, turned back and let himself in at a door behind the house. The nondescript-looking man who carried a fishing-rod, but whose sport seemed to fail just at the time that Proctor started for Frattenbury, told him this hours later. At present he made an effort to conceal his surprise and mentally said, "Damn!"

"Hallo, Mr. Colson," said Proctor cheerily, "still trying to find out about that nasty business, I suppose! You were coming to see me?"

The detective had no resource but to reply in the affirmative. This he did in a perfectly natural manner.

"Well, come along in, then," said the little man; "it's a bit chilly outside to-day."

He led the way to his bachelor dining-room, and gave the detective a chair. The latter had quite recovered his composure; in fact, outwardly, he had not shown that he had lost it.

"Just two or three things I should like to ask you, Mr. Proctor. I know you're on the jury, of course, but I won't interfere with your prerogatives. I rather wish you'd have been summoned as a witness instead."

"That was the fault of the police," said Proctor, shrugging his shoulders. "Now, what can I tell you? Stop. Have a cigar first. I can offer you a really good smoke."

"Cheek," thought Colson.

Proctor went to a cupboard by the side of the fire-place, took a bunch of keys from his pocket and unlocked it. On a shelf were more than a dozen boxes of cigars. Colson eyed them eagerly, but was too far off to see them closely, and too wise to give himself away by moving.

The little man carefully selected a box, shut the cupboard and locked it, put the box in front of Colson on the table and said:

"I think you'll like these. Now, then, Mr. Colson?"

The detective had taken out his pocket-book and was apparently consulting it closely. In reality he was inventing questions.

"We're not at all satisfied, sir," he said. "You've got a good view of the estuary. You didn't notice any other strange craft besides the *Firefly* about at the time the murder took place?"

"No, I didn't."

"It's as well to be certain. I suppose a small boat *could* have got up from lower down the estuary that night?"

"Yes—certainly. The tide was flowing, you know."

"And she could have got back?"

"There was no wind. It would have been hard rowing—unless whoever he was waited till the tide turned."

The detective asked several more questions and spoilt three or four pages of his notebook by writing down replies. Then the little man said:

"I'm just going to have tea. Won't you have some."

"Oh, thank you very much, if it's not troubling you."

"Not at all—if you don't mind excusing me for a few minutes. I've a letter to write—in my den. I want to catch the only outgoing post we have."

"Oh, certainly, sir."

"What a stroke of luck!" exclaimed the detective when Proctor had left the room. "I should hardly have believed it; but, of course, he doesn't know. He's out of his reckoning—thinks because that band was changed that we don't suspect anything."

For a minute Colson sat still, smoking his cigar. Then, with a careful look around, he crossed on tiptoe to the cupboard, took his skeleton keys from his pocket, cautiously inserted first one, then another in the keyhole and opened it.

Swiftly he ran his eye over the array of boxes. Removing a pile in front, his face beamed as he caught sight of an unfastened box in the back tier. He recognised the label. Quickly he opened it, took out a cigar and looked at the band.

"It's the one!" he murmured.

He dropped the cigar in his pocket, closed and locked the cupboard, resumed his seat, and was innocently reading a newspaper he had picked off the table, when Proctor returned, followed by his maid bringing in the tea.

"Sorry to keep you waiting," said the little man genially. "Do you take sugar, Mr. Colson?"

They chatted on various topics, and when the detective rose to go, Proctor accompanied him to the door.

"Thank you very much, Mr. Proctor."

"Not at all. Only too glad to have been of any use to you. See you to-morrow at the adjourned inquest, I suppose?"

"Yes," said Colson, "we shall meet at the inquest. Good afternoon, sir."

There was nothing further to detain him at Marsh Quay, so he went back to Frattenbury and had a long conversation with the superintendent.

"Excellent," said the latter, ticking off items on his fingers as he spoke. "The same brand of cigar, and the cablegram from Cuba tells us they have sent him these from time to time, and the firm in London corroborate it."

"And he's been in Switzerland," added Colson.

"And he's been in Switzerland," echoed the superintendent. "It's quite enough to go upon. I'll make out the deposition, and then—after the inquest."

"After the inquest," the detective said with a chuckle. "I wonder what sort of a verdict the foreman will persuade the jury to return!"

"Wilful murder—against some person unknown," replied the superintendent sardonically.

"But it won't be a true verdict," said Colson with decision.

CHAPTER XVI.
Mr. Proctor Upsets Matters

The coroner, in re-opening the inquiry, intimated that only one witness of any importance would be heard, and that, with the full consent of the police, who would not, he understood, ask for a further adjournment, the jury would be called upon to record their verdict that afternoon.

The first witness called was a postman who gave evidence that he had seen the deceased coming out of the Cathedral precincts at Frattenbury between half-past eight and nine on the Saturday evening. He, the witness, was standing outside the post office, opposite the gateway into the Close, where there was an electric lamp.

"Why did you not tell us this at the commencement of the inquiry?" asked the coroner.

"Because it was only through a portrait of the deceased, published in a newspaper afterwards, that I remembered his face, sir."

"Very well. Did you see which way he went when he came out of the Close?"

"Up the street, towards the Cross, sir."

"That was all you noticed?"

"Yes, sir, nothing more."

"Thank you."

Isaac Moss was called next. He was terribly nervous, and gave his evidence in such a low tone of voice that the coroner had frequently to ask him to speak up. Bit by bit the story he had told the superintendent and Colson was painfully dragged from him. The jury listened attentively, and evidently one or two of them were not much struck with his veracity. The coroner then questioned him.

"Why didn't you inform the police at the time?"

"I was too much frightened."

"You know that you put yourself in a very serious position, Mr. Moss?"

"Yes, I know that. I regret it very much now."

"You say that it was after half-past twelve when you crossed the estuary?"

"It was; it struck one just after I had left the yacht."

"Have you anyone who can corroborate your statement that you had not left your house before?"

"My wife is here, and my housekeeper, who brought in some hot water for my whisky just before eleven o'clock."

"We will hear them—for your sake," said the coroner. "But in any case, it is my duty to reprimand you seriously for your foolish behaviour."

Mrs. Moss and the housekeeper having given brief evidence, a juror said:

"May I ask you a question, sir?"

The coroner nodded.

"Isn't it a fact that the doctor who examined the body told us last time that the murder *might* have been committed after midnight?"

"That is so," replied the coroner, looking round. "The doctor is here. Would you like him to repeat his statement?"

"If you please, sir."

And the doctor said:

"Yes. I certainly stated that the murder might have been committed after twelve, but not long after. The probability is that it took place before that hour. Rigor mortis was palpably developed."

"Thank you," said the coroner. "Are there any more witnesses?"

There was only Joe Thatcher, who gave brief evidence as to seeing Moss board the yacht, and gave no little amusement at his indignantly assumed innocence when questioned as to his doings that night. The police were careful to state that he had come forward voluntarily.

The coroner summed up briefly, not too greatly in favour of Moss, and directed the jury to find their verdict.

"Do you wish to retire, gentlemen?"

"Yes, sir," said the juryman who had spoken before.

The jury went into another room, and there was a little buzz of conversation. The coroner did not join in it. He was absorbed in his notes. Anthony Crosby, who was seated next to the Chief Constable, said to the latter:

"I should like to call at the police station for a short conversation. There's something I want to see."

"You shall," said the Chief Constable. "I'll motor you back in my car. Norton and Colson are coming in the other. We shall probably have some interesting information to give you by that time," he went on grimly. "There are going to be developments."

"Really?"

Major Renshaw nodded.

"You'll see," he said. "I hope the jury won't be long—though it really doesn't matter what verdict they bring in. I say—you won't mind waiting a few minutes before we start back?"

"Oh, dear, no."

But the jury still remained out of the room. Presently a note was handed in and given to the coroner, who opened it, read it and then said:

"The jury wish to know whether the police are satisfied with the evidence of Mr. Moss."

He glanced at Moss as he spoke. The Jew's face paled. The superintendent whispered a word or two to him, and the Chief Constable said to the coroner:

"You may tell the jury, sir, that we are perfectly satisfied. We have nothing to bring against Mr. Moss."

Moss gave a sigh of relief, and the coroner scribbled a note to the jury. In about ten minutes' time that body filed in, one or two of them looking very heated.

The coroner addressed the foreman.

"Are you all agreed on your verdict?"

"We are, sir."

"And it is?"

"Wilful murder against some person or persons unknown."

"Very well. I agree with your finding. The inquiry is closed."

After a few brief formalities the assembly broke up. Major Renshaw, the superintendent and Colson detached themselves from the rest and went outside the inn. Presently Proctor came out and was walking across to his house opposite, when the Chief Constable spoke to him.

"We have a matter of business with you that is best discussed in private, Mr. Proctor. May we come over to your house?"

He looked at the three men steadily, smiled slightly and said:

"By all means, Major. Come along." As they walked across he said to them, in quite a matter-of-fact way: "I had quite a little trouble with that jury. Two or three of them were bent on returning a verdict against the unfortunate Moss. Of course, he didn't do it, but it wasn't till we had the note from the coroner that they fell in with the rest."

"No—he didn't do it," said the Major dryly.

The little man was opening his front door. He gave the Chief Constable a quick glance, pursed up his mouth and smiled. He led the way into the dining-room. The three policemen were silent. Then Major Renshaw addressed him, his face very grave.

"Mr. Proctor, I fear I have a most unpleasant du——"

"I know exactly what you're going to do," broke in the little man before the other could go on. "You're going to arrest me for the murder of Reginald Templeton, and then warn me that anything I say may be used as evidence against me. Isn't that so?"

For a moment or two Major Renshaw was silent with astonishment. The superintendent gave a low whistle. Colson exclaimed:

"Great Scott!"

The Chief Constable recovered himself.

"You are right, Mr. Proctor," he said sternly. "Take care what you say, sir!" For Proctor was again about to speak, and he did speak, in spite of the warning.

"One minute, Major—I beg of you, one minute. Oh, you may make use of anything I say, and welcome. But it's for your own sake. I've a strong respect for the police. I knew you were going to arrest me. I expected it before this."

"You are only doing yourself harm, sir!" thundered the Chief Constable in his best military style. "I warn you."

"And I warn you, Major," said the imperturbable little man, pointing at the Chief Constable, "if you once formally arrest me, I shall remain silent until I'm before the magistrates. And then you and your police will be a laughing-stock. And I shan't even have to employ a lawyer. It's true, Major."

The astonished Chief Constable hesitated. He turned to the superintendent, but the latter only shook his head in bewilderment.

Colson was hard at work biting his finger-nails. It was an unprecedented scene.

"What do you mean, sir?" asked the Chief Constable, hesitating a little.

"This, Major. I'll go with you to Frattenbury with pleasure, and you can detain me till you're satisfied. I'll explain everything, and you may arrest me if you like when I've finished—though you won't. But if you do it now—I'm dumb."

The Major took the superintendent to the other end of the room and held a whispered conversation with him. Proctor calmly lighted a cigar and handed his case to Colson. The latter refused it with a shake of the head, and the little man only grinned exasperatingly at him.

Then the Major came forward.

"Very well, Mr. Proctor," he said stiffly, "we will take you into Frattenbury, please, on detention for the present. But I warn you that there are ugly facts against you."

"I know there are," said Proctor coolly, "and I was a bit glad to hear that Jew's evidence just now—and to hear the doctor repeat his. But I've nothing to be afraid of. I'm quite ready, Major."

It was when they arrived at the police station that Proctor explained. Crosby was present. The Chief Constable had told him something about the affair as he motored him into Frattenbury.

"You may as well hear what he's got to say," he said.

Proctor was accommodated with a chair in the private office at the police station. The superintendent sat at his desk, pen in hand. Major Renshaw began:

"Now, Mr. Proctor, we will hear what you have to say, if you please."

"Very well, Major. Will you kindly send for Mr. Stephen Merrifield? His place of business is just opposite here."

"The corn merchant?"

"Exactly. You'll take his word, I suppose?"

Without replying the Major sent for Merrifield. The little man went on:

"When I first had a notion that you were suspecting me, Mr. Colson," he said, addressing the detective, "was that Monday morning when I recovered my canoe. My nephew told me what you had asked him about disturbing me in the dark hours, and so on, and I knew you wouldn't have said it without some reason. Also, I saw you were interested in that canoe being taken away—though for the life of me I can't guess why. I put two and two together and came to the conclusion that you were trying to find out whether I had run off with my own canoe, and left it where it was pretty sure Phil would find it in the morning. And it puzzled me. But it also put me on my guard."

"Go on," said the superintendent.

"Well, then came the inquest. When the doctor said that death might have occurred after midnight, I was just a little perturbed—you'll see why presently. I suppose I was the nearest person to Templeton—his yacht lay just opposite my house. And when Canon Fittleworth handed in that cigar band, for the moment I was fairly alarmed."

"That's why you cha——" began the superintendent, but Colson stopped him with a warning gesticulation.

"Eh?" asked Proctor.

"Oh—nothing," said the superintendent. "Go on, please."

"Although the Canon stated the cigar was one of his own special brand, I knew I had the same brand in my house. Why," he said to the superintendent, "you smoked one yourself—on the Sunday morning, and remarked how good it was. Don't you remember?"

"I do," said the superintendent, "but I never noticed the band."

"I was wondering if you had," went on Proctor, with a smile. "Then I wanted the coroner to put a question to the Canon, but he wouldn't allow it."

"What was the question?" asked Major Renshaw.

"I only wanted him to ask whether the Canon could remember to whom he gave any of his cigars. But I concluded afterwards that you would examine the reverend gentleman pretty closely on that point. I gather you *did*, and came to the conclusion that it wasn't in that quarter that you had to make your investigations."

"Meanwhile," said Major Renshaw, "knowing you possessed the same brand of cigar, and in order to put us off your track——"

But he was interrupted. A newcomer was shown in, a portly man with grey moustache and short beard and a round, jovial face.

"Oh, good afternoon, Mr. Merrifield," said the Chief Constable. "Do you mind waiting just a minute?"

"Certainly, sir." He looked round the room, nodded affably to Mr. Proctor, and took the seat which Colson offered him.

"Go on, Mr. Proctor."

"Where was I? Oh, yes—I know. Well, very soon after the inquest, I found I was being watched. That wasn't much of a fisherman you sent over to Marsh Quay, Mr. Colson! Oh, yes, I knew. When I went over to Portsmouth last Monday on business, and found that this fisherman travelled by the same train there and back, I was pretty certain."

"We were bound to keep an eye on you," said the superintendent.

"I don't dispute it. But I'm afraid, as an innocent man, I resented it. My way of looking at it was that I'd have liked you to come and have the whole thing out with me. Of course, you know your own methods best. Anyhow, yesterday I set a little trap for you, Mr. Colson. I hope you'll forgive me."

"A trap?" said Colson.

"In this way. I saw you lounging about at Marsh Quay. I imagined you wanted me out of the way, so I started for Frattenbury. But I very soon retraced my steps, and let myself in at the back door. Out of the window I saw you in my garden. I came out and asked you in. Then I made an excuse for leaving you in my dining-room, which was what you wanted, I imagine."

Colson looked very black, especially as the superintendent gave him an amused glance.

"Well," went on the little man, "while you were examining the contents of my cigar cupboard I was watching you from outside, through the window. I was behind the laurel bush opposite it! You took one of those cigars. I'd counted 'em first. So I guessed you were going to arrest me pretty soon."

"That's all very well, so far as it goes," said the Chief Constable, "but it's only your own story. It doesn't in any way clear you."

"I know. But you'll soon be satisfied. In the first place, the evidence of Isaac Moss—which you allow—proves that the crime was committed before one o'clock on the Sunday morning, eh, Major?"

"Yes, I concede that."

"Very well. Now will you hear what Mr. Merrifield has to say?"

Merrifield was just going to speak, but the Chief Constable held up his hand for silence.

"What do you wish me to ask him, Mr. Proctor?"

"Where I was on the Saturday night."

"If you know that, Mr. Merrifield, perhaps you'll tell us?"

"Why, of course I will. You don't mean to say you've been thinking my friend here committed a murder? Why, he wouldn't hurt a fly! It's all right, Major Renshaw. Mr. Proctor had supper in my house on the Saturday night in question. He and my wife and a friend staying with us played bridge afterwards, and I'm ashamed to say we went on into Sunday morning. It was close on one o'clock when we finished the last rubber. It's a lonesome sort of a walk to Marsh Quay, so I offered to run Mr. Proctor back in my car—and did."

The superintendent brought his hand down on the desk.

"That explains what Joe Thatcher said about a motor!" he exclaimed. "Well, Mr. Merrifield?"

"That's all there is, Superintendent. It didn't take long to get down there. I stopped the car opposite his gate, and he asked me to go in. I went, and I don't deny that we had a final whisky and soda to wind up the evening. It was exactly half-past one by the clock on his mantelpiece when I went out and came back to Frattenbury. I hope that satisfies you?"

"Am I to be set at liberty?" asked Proctor dryly.

The little man looked so quaint, with his bald, egg-shaped head, that Major Renshaw could scarcely restrain a smile.

"There's nothing else we can do with you, Mr. Proctor. But I wish you had told us all this before."

Proctor drew himself up with an air of injured dignity.

"I objected to being shadowed," he said. "It put my back up. You'll confess it wouldn't have been wise to have arrested me?"

"Ah, don't say any more, Mr. Proctor. We'll try to forgive you this time. I'm sorry we've upset you, but we're quite satisfied now."

"You don't want me any longer, Major?" asked Merrifield. "All right. Come along, Proctor, old chap. You'll be wanting something to pick you up after all this, and I've got it at my house."

When they were gone the Major, the superintendent and Anthony Crosby looked at each other for a moment or two, and then simultaneously burst into a roar of laughter. But Colson did not join in. His face was as black as a thunder-cloud.

"Come," said Crosby to the Chief Constable, "you'll admit he fairly had you, Major Renshaw? Aren't you glad you didn't arrest him?"

"I am," said the Major grimly. "I confess it. Conceited little beggar! I'm glad he had a fright, though. He did, you know, or he wouldn't have changed that cigar band at the inquest."

"Ah," said the lawyer reflectively, "it was only natural, I suppose. A sudden impulse, you know. I can quite understand that even an innocent man, suddenly confronted with such a damning bit of evidence against him, should succumb to the temptation and take advantage of his peculiar opportunity. How do you think he did it?"

"I know," said Colson gloomily—"there were several bands from Grayson's cigars lying in the grate. He picked up one of those. I remembered afterwards—I could almost swear I saw him do it. That was what put us on to Grayson. We've taken all three suspects—and now there's an end of them."

The Chief Constable, beneath his somewhat stiff military bearing, was a kindly man. He put his hand on the detective's shoulder.

"Come, Colson," he said, "you couldn't help it. It's a bit of a set-back, I know; but after all, it's cleared the ground."

Colson looked up, and blurted out what was on his mind:

"Are you going to call in Scotland Yard, sir?"

The superintendent looked hard at Major Renshaw, but said nothing. The Major reflected. Then he said:

"You shall have another week, Colson. Get on with the job and see what you can do."

"Thank you, sir."

"Look here," broke in Crosby. "I've got a train to catch, and I'd almost forgotten—I want to have a look at that blotting-pad. I've got the copy, but I want to see the original."

The superintendent produced it. The lawyer took it to the light, pulled a big magnifying glass out a of his pocket, and examined it carefully.

"Ah!" he exclaimed, "my guess is correct. Who made the copy?"

"I did," said Colson.

"You've left out something. Look here—through my glass. Take that word ICES. Do you notice, first of all, that there's a slightly bigger space between the E and the S than there is between the other letters?"

"Y-e-s," admitted the detective.

"And can you see, with the help of the glass, anything between the E and the S?"

"There's the faintest little mark—not between them, but just over the space."

"Exactly. And that's a comma—an apostrophe. It isn't EZRA'S ICES at all; it's EZRA, then three spaces, then ICE'S. The first space represents the division between the two words, so we want two letters before ICES. EZRA being a Christian name, it follows in all probability that the other is a surname. Now, what surnames of five letters end in ICE? Take the supposition first, that the second missing letter is a vowel. You might have 'Daice,' 'Laice,' 'Maice'—they don't look likely, eh?—or 'Reice,' or 'Joice'—generally spelt with a 'y'—or 'Juice.' I've tried every consonant as a first letter. Take consonants as the second letter, and put any vowels as the first, and you don't make much either. But there are just two fairly common surnames that you can get by using two consonants as the first two letters, and they are 'PRICE' and 'GRICE.' If I were working on this clue, I should go for Ezra Price or Ezra Grice."

The three men followed him closely.

"Now take the next two words, connected by the '&.' I've only time to give you a hasty deduction. There are two words which would agree with the spaces in the first word—'profession' or 'confession.' 'ROO' is at the end of the line of writing. It has obviously only one letter in front of it, and one, or perhaps two, after it. I've tried every consonant as the first letter—with only one result. And I make the word 'PROOF' or 'PROOFS.' There you are—'Ezra Price's (or Grice's) confession and proof.' It looks interesting. Whoever it was to whom Templeton wrote that letter, he knew something about Ezra Price—or Grice."

"That looks feasible," said the Chief Constable.

"I'll tell you what I'll do," went on the lawyer. "As Templeton's representative—he's made me his executor—I'll put an advertisement in the papers asking anyone who heard from him since he returned to England to communicate with me and tell me the nature of the correspondence. If a reference to this letter turns up, well and good. If not, it's a process of elimination, and we can assume that the recipient doesn't want to give it away. Let me do this—then there won't be a question of the police having anything to do with it. I must run; I've only just time to catch my train. I'll let you know the result."

CHAPTER XVII.
New Theories

"You've just got to solve it, Bob, and you're going to solve it," said Mrs. Colson that night to her somewhat disconsolate husband. "And that for two reasons: first because such a wicked wretch ought to be punished, and secondly because you're my dear hubby. So there now!"

She gave him a kiss and took a chair by him in front of the fire.

"I've got to begin all over again," he said moodily.

"Of course you have, dear. And what of that? You've ever so much better a chance now you've cleared away the hindrances. Now, let's begin. We're going to talk it over, Bob, and your wife is going to help you with her big brain—oh, ever so much!"

"Well, I've got a week's probation, so to speak," he said, "and I'll jolly well try. All right, we'll talk it over. You shall begin."

She put her elbows on her knees and rested her chin on her hands.

"First of all, then, let's get rid of all the old theories. You've gone on the supposition that the murderer was near the spot all the time, haven't you?"

"Well, it looked like it."

"I know. Now, is there anyone else living there whom you could suspect?"

By this time he had a mental category of every man, woman and child at Marsh Quay. He turned it over.

"No," he said, "only boatmen and labourers—and a retired parson who lives near, a very nice chap. Rule him out."

"Very well. Then we'll begin by assuming that the murderer came from a distance."

"Frattenbury?"

"Possibly. We'll get back to that later on. Next point—the motive. Up to now you've thought it was to get the diamonds. Let's throw that out; I'm sick of the diamonds."

"You wouldn't be if you had 'em, dear. All right, then the diamonds shall go. Let's say he was after something else."

"And that something else was Templeton's life."

"Eh?"

"Why not? There is such a thing as premeditated murder, isn't there?"

"You may be right," he assented, "or Templeton may have been possessed of something else——"

"That was worth taking his life to get! Remember *that*!" she said, lifting a warning finger. "People don't generally commit murder for the sake of killing anyone, you know. Now, let's get on. Let's try and picture how it was done."

"I told you last night how I'd worked it out, dear. The murderer went on board in the dinghy——"

"Stop, stop. Now remember, Bob, that's an old theory. Everything we discuss to-night must be a new idea. That theory presupposes that the murderer was on the yacht first. Put it away. Tell me what other alternatives were there? I'm out of my depth here."

He thought carefully for a few minutes and replied:

"Only three, as far as I can see. First, some boat from outside came in. Not likely, because one of the canoes was found unfastened in the morning. Mrs. Yates told me this. Secondly, that the murderer went out to the yacht in the canoe after Templeton had returned. Also unlikely, because he would scarcely have transferred his stick to the dinghy. Thirdly, that hardly seems probable."

"Then it's worth consideration, Bob. You've gone, too much, on probabilities. Let's have this 'thirdly,' please."

She had never heard of the theologian's famous dictum, "*Credo, quia incredibile est*," but it was the same line of reasoning.

"It's this, then. Templeton himself rowed the murderer out in the dinghy, the latter sitting in the stern and laying his stick down as he sat. They both went on board and the murder was committed. Now comes the improbable part. The murderer rowed back to shore in the dinghy, ran the canoe down to the water, paddled back towing the dinghy, made the latter fast again to the yacht, and finally returned in the canoe, dragging her up again, but forgetting to fasten her painter to the post as before."

For some minutes Mrs. Colson gazed steadily into the fire in silence. Colson refilled and lighted his pipe, and waited. Then she said:

"I see. But he might have had a very artful object in doing this. If he went on board with Templeton, and he didn't live at Marsh Quay, he must have met him somewhere else first—and gone with him. Well, if he'd only landed in the dinghy and left it on the shore, it would have been a clear proof that Templeton had taken him on board—and if, by any chance, they had happened to be seen by anybody *first*—he would naturally have been suspected. His very best plan would be to leave the dinghy fast to the yacht, and he could only have done so in the way you say."

Colson smoked for a moment or two.

"It was taking a big risk—risking time for getting clear away."

"It was worth it, Bob. Would it make much noise—getting the canoe down to the water?"

"Oh, no; it was lying on a patch of grass—the grass grows right down to the water's edge, you know—and if the tide wasn't quite up—and it wasn't—there would be soft, sandy mud just there between the green and the water's edge. The stony part of the beach is nearer the quay. And the canoe is almost light enough for a strong man to carry. No, there needn't have been any noise."

She looked at him and smiled.

"We're getting on, then."

"There's another point in favour—ah, you've scored again, dear—I was just going to say that it would make things look so improbable."

They both laughed heartily. Suddenly a little shadow came over her face.

"My dear," she said, "he's a very clever man—I'm sure he is. Do take care, Bob."

"What do you mean?"

"When you match your wits against a man like this you have to be careful. And he probably knows you're doing it."

"That's all right," he said; "he's put me down as a blunderer long ago. Remember, he knows nothing about the walking-stick or the cigar. He can't suspect."

"Don't let him, then. Well—let's follow it up. He walked out with Templeton from Frattenbury."

"What makes you say that?"

"It don't know—just because I'm a woman, and you can't expect me always to reason things out and say why. But I am going to think now—don't speak, Bob."

There was a long silence. She suddenly turned towards him, gripped his hand, and said:

"Bob!"

"What?"

"Suppose you're mistaken again! And by our plan you *are*, you know—because we're trying everything fresh."

"I don't see what——"

"Don't interrupt, dear. Suppose those stick marks were not made by Templeton going *into* Frattenbury, but were made by the murderer walking out with him."

"But that's not likely. They were on the right side of the path coming in, and——"

"You silly dear! But they were on the left-hand side going out. Bob—look out for a left-handed man!"

"By Jove!" he exclaimed, "there's something in that. In that case Templeton *carried* his stick in with him and didn't put it to the ground."

"Was he short or tall?"

"Medium—inclined to be short."

She clapped her hands.

"That's it, dear!—look out for a tall, left-handed man. If only you could find out whether Templeton *carried* his stick—for certain——?"

"Stop—stop a bit!"

He got up and paced the little room, smoking furiously.

"I know!" he exclaimed, stopping suddenly. "There *is* a chance of finding out. If only he remembers."

"Who?"

"I won't tell you till I'm certain. Go on, dear."

She waited a little.

"I can't think of any more, Bob. Is there anything else *new*—anything, I mean, that you haven't followed up yet?"

"There's that blotting-pad," he said. "I don't know that there's anything in it——"

"Then for goodness' sake follow it up, Bob. That's what I *mean*."

"Well, the lawyer from London, Mr. Crosby, gave me a hint about that. I'll tell you."

He produced his copy and showed her what Crosby had pointed out.

"Ezra Price—or Ezra Grice," she said, "let's take it then. How would you work on it?"

After a bit he said:

"Well, the only way is this. If we take the letter at all as part of the business, and fit it in with these new theories, we must assume that the man to whom it was written knows something about Ezra. And we are assuming that this man lives—or was at the time—in Frattenbury. But I've never heard the name of Ezra—Price or Grice."

"But you've only lived in Frattenbury six years, dear. Of course you can't expect to have heard of him. Can't you find out if he was ever here, or if anyone knew anything about him?"

"I might," he said. "Mr. Buckland, the chemist, has got a pretty fair memory of all kinds of people. He's lived here all his life. We often go to him when we want to find out the past of anyone. I'll try him to-morrow."

She jumped up from her seat. "I'm going to get supper now, Bob. We've done enough for to-night. Yes, we'll have it early because you're going to be a nice old dear and take me to the pictures, and forget there was ever a murder at Marsh Quay and a detective who did his best, and then—even though he was a brainy, oh, ever so clever a man, and wanted to be an inspector one day—had to take his little wife's advice, and pay for it in kisses—oh—that's enough, Bob—it wasn't worth *all* those."

"The overplus were for yourself," said Colson, "and I still owe a heavy bill."

Next day Colson, in a far more cheery mood, after seeing Constable Gadsden for a moment and consulting the latter's ponderous and well-thumbed notebook, cycled once more on the now familiar road to Marsh Quay, where he inquired at a cottage for one George Simmonds, and was told by his wife that he was helping to load the *Lucy*, which had returned once more for a cargo of gravel. He very soon found the man and said to him:

"Have you got a good memory, Simmonds?"

"I remember the last man as stood me a pint o' beer, guv'nor," was the response.

"Well, perhaps you'll have the same cause to remember me when we've finished. Anyhow, on the morning when the murder was discovered here you told the police-constable you'd met Mr. Templeton the previous afternoon—going into Frattenbury."

"That's right, guv'nor. 'Twarn't he as give me that pint, though."

"Quite so. Now, let's see if you can tell me how he was dressed."

The man described him pretty accurately.

"Good," said the detective; "had he got anything in his hand?"

The man thought a moment.

"Yes—a stick. I didn't take no notice on it, though—I can't say what 'twas like."

"Never mind that. Was he carrying it or walking with it?"

Simmonds grinned sheepishly and shook his head.

"Look here," said Colson, picking up a bit of stick that was lying on the ground, "this is what I mean. Did he hold it by the handle and stick it in the ground like *this*—or carry it, by the middle, *so*?"

"Oh, I can easily tell 'ee that. He had it by the middle, same as you have now."

"You're sure?"

"Sartain, guv'nor—I see him a-doin' on it."

"All right. Here you are then."

The man spat on the coin, pocketed it, and grinned.

"Thankee, guv'nor—that's good for a quart, that is. I shan't forget *you*—if anyone wants to pay me for rememberin'."

"*One* to the wife," said Colson as he sped back to Frattenbury. "Now for Mr. Buckland."

He found the chemist standing behind his counter, a grave-looking man with wrinkled forehead and a big walrus moustache.

"I want a bit of information, if you can give it to me, Mr. Buckland."

"Certainly. Come inside, won't you?"

"Inside" was a tiny, dingy parlour at the back of the shop. The chemist closed the door.

"Well, Mr. Colson?"

"You know most people who've lived here the last forty years, Mr. Buckland. Did you ever hear of anyone by the name of Ezra Price?"

"Ezra Price," reflected the chemist—"the name has a sort of familiar sound. There aren't many Ezras about, either. Ezra *Price*—it—somehow doesn't seem right—yet——"

"Ezra Grice, then."

"Ezra *Grice*—that seems more like it—yes—now let me think—it must have been a long time ago——Grice—yes—I know now. He was a lawyer's clerk—or something—I'm beginning to remember—a bad lot, wasn't he? I'm not sure. Stop, though—I know who'd tell you more about him. He was in Mr. Norwood's office—so far as I can recollect."

"Mr. Norwood?"

"That's it—you'd better try him."

"All right, I will," said the detective. "Thank you very much for putting me on the scent."

"Not at all."

As he passed down the street, however, he saw Mr. Norwood hurrying into the Magistrates' Court which was then sitting. So, wishing to see him at leisure, he called at the lawyer's house in the evening, when he felt pretty certain of finding him at home. He waited in the hall while the maid tapped at the dining-room door and announced him.

"Oh—show him in here," came a voice from the room.

Francis Norwood had just finished his solitary dinner and was draining his glass of port.

"Good evening, sergeant," he said in his formal manner. "Something you want to see me about? Another inquest?"

"No, sir. But I thought you could give me some information—I was told you could. I understand there was a young man employed by you—many years ago."

"I've employed a number of young men in my time—some of them to my cost! What was his name?"

"Ezra Grice, sir."

"Oh—oh—yes, I think I remember him. Of course I do."

He reached for the decanter, noticed it was empty, and said:

"I was going to offer you a glass of port, sergeant, but I see there's none left. Will you have a whisky and soda?"

"Thank you, sir."

Francis Norwood rose stiffly from his chair and opened the door of a sideboard just behind him.

"Tut, tut!" he exclaimed, "there isn't any decanter—oh, here's a bottle."

He took a corkscrew from a drawer and drew the cork from the bottle, Colson looking on in silence. Then he produced two tumblers and poured whisky into both, filling them up with soda.

One he gave to Colson, and the other he kept for himself. First taking a drink from it, he said:

"Well, now, I dare say I can help you. May I ask what you want to know about Ezra Grice?"

"Eh? Oh—yes. Anything you can tell me, sir."

"And why?"

"It concerns a case we have in hand, sir."

Colson never gave anything away if he could help it.

"I see. Well, it's years ago now—quite twenty years, sergeant. Grice was my clerk. He must have been three or four and twenty at the time. A sharp young fellow. His parents kept a little bookshop in the North Street—they're both dead now. Do you want to know why he left me?"

"If you please, sir."

"I'm sorry to say I had to dismiss him; I ought to have prosecuted him, but I didn't. He robbed me, sergeant. For the sake of his parents, who were respectable people and implored me not to put him in prison, I spared him. He left Frattenbury at once, and, so far as I know, he's never entered it again."

"Do you know where he went?"

"I believe he emigrated—the best thing he could do. But, mind you, I've never seen him since."

"Have you ever heard of him, sir?"

"In a way. A rumour reached me some time ago that he was dead, but I can't vouch for it."

"We should like to get hold of him if he's alive," said the detective, after a short pause.

The lawyer took a sip at his glass, and replied in his dry, precise manner:

"If you really want him, sergeant, I'd do anything I can in the matter. Why not advertise for him? You're quite welcome to use my name in an advertisement—unless you think if he *is* alive and sees the advertisement it might frighten him? But, pray do what you think best. If you like to step into my office in the morning I can show you his record—and I may have notes about him you might like to see. Any way, I'm quite at your service."

"That is very kind of you, sir. We may try advertising."

"Do—by all means. I hope it may be successful—if you want him. Good evening, sergeant. Come to my office in the morning, then."

When the detective had departed, the lawyer lighted a cigarette and slowly finished his whisky; then he took up a newspaper he had laid down on the table when Colson came in, and was studying it when the maid announced:

"Dr. Hazell, sir."

"Come in, Hazell."

The little doctor entered. He was a bit flustered.

"Good evening, Norwood. I haven't come in to stay. I say, you remember when I was dining here some nights back Sir Peter told us about 'Virginian Reefs'—said they were good, don't you know?"

"Well?"

"I hope to the Lord you won't get any, Norwood."

The lawyer laughed his dry, short laugh.

"Why?"

"I was fool enough to buy five hundred of 'em, and they're down to fifteen shillings in to-night's paper."

"Perhaps they'll pick up," said Norwood. "Sir Peter seemed to think so."

"The worst of it is there's another report. Not the one Sir Peter spoke of, you know—and it's a bad one. I can't afford to lose the money—I shall have to cut the loss. I've been a damn fool, Norwood."

"I'm sorry," said the lawyer, "but I'm afraid you have."

"Well, at all events, I thought I'd warn you. Good night. I've got a patient to see."

"Good night, Doctor. Thank you very much."

Meanwhile, Colson was making his way to the police station, which was at the bottom of the South Street. He seemed a little lost in thought, for he nearly ran into Canon Fittleworth, who was coming out of the Close to post a letter.

"Oh," said the Canon, recognising him, "have you got five minutes to spare? Thanks. If you don't mind coming round to my house a minute, I've got that list ready."

"I should like to have it very much, sir," replied Colson.

The worthy Canon prided himself on his accuracy of detail. In his study he produced his list.

"Mrs. Fittleworth and my daughter have carefully refreshed my memory," he said. "Half a dozen times we've gone over all the men who dined here—or smoked with me—since I received that box of cigars. Here's the list. I hope it won't help you in one way—I mean, they are all my intimate friends!"

He handed a paper to the detective, who ran his eye down the names eagerly. They were all prominent Frattenbury gentlemen—Dr. Hazell, Sir Peter Birchnall, Cathedral dignitaries, and so on.

"I suppose you can't remember if anyone here took away a cigar without smoking it, sir?"

"Yes, I can," said the Canon. "One of them who was dining here a few weeks ago was so struck with the flavour, that I gave him a dozen of them—put 'em in an empty box, and he took them with him."

"Indeed. Who was he?"

And the Canon replied dryly, a twinkle in his eye:

"The Dean!"

Colson waited till he got outside the house. Then he said what he thought:

"Damn these parsons!"

CHAPTER XVIII.
Sir James Perrivale's Story

The advertisement inquiring for news of the whereabouts of Ezra Grice, some time of Frattenbury, was duly inserted in *The Times* and other daily papers. The Chief Constable demurred a little at first, but finally agreed with Colson that there might be something in it, although, after the lapse of such a long period, the discovery of the individual in question had many chances against it.

At the end of the week Colson had a letter from Anthony Crosby, in which he said:

My advertisement for any correspondents of the late Mr. Templeton has had few results, and I send you them for what they are worth. I have, for convenience's sake, tabulated them as follows:

1. Two letters written to friends at his club—one from Salcombe and another from Poole—ordinary letters stating he was shortly coming up to London.

2. Four letters to tradesmen, ordering certain goods.

3. A letter to the editor of a magazine of travel, arranging for the publication of an article.

Neither of these, for I have made inquiries, refers to the matter of Ezra Grice. We may, therefore, build upon the elimination theory, and presume that if the recipient of the letter has seen my advertisement he prefers to say nothing about it.

I notice that you are advertising for this man Grice. If it will help you, I am willing to offer a reward of £50 for information which may produce him. Pray use your discretion in this matter when you re-advertise.

I think I have now succeeded in piecing together the whole of the blotting-pad letter. You have probably arrived at a similar conclusion. Some may be guess-work, but I am inclined to believe that it reads thus:

"hand over Ezra Grice's confession & proof.
This is final."

Of course it is only a bit of the whole letter, but it is not without interest.

The police were debating as to whether they should take advantage of the lawyer's offer of the reward, when a tall, weather-beaten individual, with a close-cropped moustache, got out of the London train at Frattenbury and inquired his way to the police head-quarters. He was dressed in a loose knickerbocker suit of excellent West End cut, and walked with the air of a man of resource and authority. He sent in his card and asked to see the superintendent of police.

"Sir James Perrivale," read the superintendent. "The name seems familiar. Show him in, Peters."

"Good morning," said Sir James. "I've called about that advertisement—you know, what?"

"Advertisement?"

"The what-d'ye-call-it—that fellow named Grice. I saw the thing in my club yesterday."

"Pray sit down, Sir James. We shall be glad if you can give us any information about him."

"Look here, Superintendent, I want to know what you want him for. Anything against him? The poor devil's gone through enough already. What?"

"We don't know anything against him, but we certainly want to find out about him."

"Wasn't it down here somewhere that poor Templeton was murdered?"

"Yes, Sir James—about two miles off."

"Queer coincidence, what? Perhaps that's what you want him for?"

"I don't understand, Sir James."

"Eh? Oh, I thought perhaps you knew Grice was with him in South Africa."

"Was he, by George?" exclaimed the superintendent. "We never knew that. We only wish we had more details about Mr. Templeton; it might help us. Do you know anything?"

"Oh, Lord, no! Only I knew Templeton—over the water, and Grice too, and I was interested, what?"

"Will you tell us what you know?"

"Of course I will. Want me to make a statement? All right. Well, I've only just got back from South Africa. Been doing a bit of big-game shooting up country—I'm speaking of three or four months ago. I had a camp up beyond the Umbrati river, and Templeton struck it. He was on his way back. Queer chap, you know. Used to go and bury himself for a couple o' years in the interior—exploring. Well, as I was saying, he struck our camp. He was in a pretty low way, too, only a few of his natives and this chap Grice left—very little ammunition. Clothes like a scarecrow."

"What was Grice doing with him?"

"He'd taken him, see? Grice had been in the country years—Boer War, trading, diamond finding, ivory—all sorts of things. Sort o' chap down on his luck and then up again. But he knew a lot—he was a useful man. Spoke most of the dialects and understood handling natives. Templeton picked him up at Johannesburg, and got him to go with him. Poor wretch! Never thought he'd bring him back."

"What was the matter?"

"Lots. Broken arm, fever, and all sorts of complications. They'd had to carry him on a stretcher for a week or more. Thin as a lath. I had a few drugs—they'd nothing left—and did what I could. But he looked like pegging out pretty soon."

"Did he?"

"I'll tell you. Templeton, you see, was in a hurry to get on. Don't wonder. Grice was at death's door, and he had to leave him. There was something or other first—Grice's will, I fancy. Anyhow, Templeton was with him a long time the day before he left, and then called me and Ottery—Colonel Ottery, you know, who was shooting with me—to witness Grice's signature.

"The next morning Templeton left. We'd rigged him out a bit, and gave him what we could spare. We knew he'd be all right. I promised him I'd give Grice a decent burial."

"And——"

"No, we didn't. One of my men—Zulu, he was—asked to take him in hand—uncle had been a medicine man, and he knew something about it, what? Queer things they know sometimes about herbs and so on, pretend they're magic, of course. The poor wretch was so far gone that it didn't seem to matter, so I let the chap take him in hand. Poured a scalding hot drink down his throat, put white powder in his eyes—rubbed him down—all sorts of things. But it answered. Before we broke up that camp, Superintendent, Grice was walking about again."

"What happened to him?"

"I brought him down to Cape Town and set him on his legs. He'd got a bit of cash. Templeton had paid him a lump sum down before he took him, and he'd banked it. Anyhow, he said he should stay at Cape Town for a bit till he was strong again—so there he is."

"Sir James," said the superintendent, "I'm most greatly obliged to you—more than I can say. But we must have Grice here—as soon as possible. How shall we get him?"

"You haven't a charge against him?"

"No, no. It's not a question of bringing him over on an extradition warrant. He must come of his own accord. We want him at once. But there's a difficulty."

"What's that, eh?"

"He left this town twenty years ago, when he got into trouble. He was not prosecuted, but it might make him suspicious."

Sir James Perrivale thought a moment.

"Tell me, Superintendent, in confidence, of course, is it anything to do with Templeton's murder, because it looks like it to me, what?"

"Yes, it is. Grice may help us materially in getting on the track of our man. That's why we want him."

"Tell you what, then. I always liked Templeton—queer chap though he was. I'll help you. Grice will listen to me. I'll cable for him to come over by the next boat—and cable him the passage."

"If it's a question of expense, Sir James——"

"No, no. I'd like to. Leave it to me. I'll get him for you. And now I'm here you might do something for me. I've read about the murder, of course. How can I get to the place to have a look at it? Morbid curiosity, what?"

"I'll run you down now in a car, with pleasure."

When they arrived at Marsh Quay it was peaceful enough. The tide was in, bathed in a sunshine splendour. Sir James remarked:

"Queer, isn't it? Here's this chap Templeton, risked his life over and over again, all sorts of adventures, escapes, and so on, and he gets done to death in a quiet, beautiful spot like this—in the midst of our civilisation, what? Gad, I wonder who did it? I mustn't ask what you know?"

"You may ask, Sir James. But I can't tell you—only—I think things are beginning to move. Did you know Mr. Templeton well?"

"Met him several times—here and abroad," said Sir James, as they turned away from the water's edge. "Nobody knew him well; he wasn't that sort. And nobody I ever met could turn him if he'd once made up his mind to do a thing—and he did queer things at times. If he thought a course was right, he'd stick to it—conventionality and advice and prudence be damned! I shouldn't wonder if it wasn't something of this kind that brought that knife into his heart."

Sir James went away, promising to let the superintendent know how things were shaping, and the latter rang up Colson, who was in his house. He went to the police station at once, and listened attentively to the story, but made little comment.

He was still working more or less in the dark and was puzzled. But he acknowledged that the prospect was brighter.

As he went up the street afterwards, he met Francis Norwood coming out of the bank. The lawyer stopped him.

"Well, sergeant. I've seen your advertisements. Have you found Ezra Grice?"

"No, sir," said Colson truthfully, for he had not found him.

"I see. Well, as I said before—anything I can do, you know."

"Thank you, sir."

The detective stood, lost in thought, as Norwood went on his way—looking at him. Then he shook his head slowly, went back to the police station, asked for the copy of the proceedings at the inquest, took it home and studied it till his wife literally dragged him out of his chair to come to the meal. But he was very silent as he ate, and as soon as the meal was over, returned to his perusal of the report. Then he took out his notebook and made quite long entries.

CHAPTER XIX.
Colson Makes an Appointment

Anthony Crosby, busy man as he was, found a little time to follow up, from a natural curiosity, the strange letter that Reginald Templeton had addressed to him. As the letter had surmised, this was not very difficult to do. He consulted several old law lists, and made certain inquiries at the office of the Law Society in Chancery Lane.

The result was that he went to the newspaper reading-room, of the British Museum, where he had a reader's ticket, applied for files of newspapers twenty years old, and very soon made himself acquainted with the charge that had been brought against Winnie's father all those years ago. He shook his head as he read the case—embezzlement of clients' monies.

"No wonder Templeton advised her mother to keep it from the girl," he murmured. "No—there is no occasion to tell her now—— Hallo! That's curious!"

He read on carefully, then gave back the file of papers to the attendant. As he walked away he said to himself:

"This chap Ezra Grice is a bit of a puzzle. I wonder what Templeton knew about him? I think I'll run down to Frattenbury and have a talk with the Chief Constable; it's better than writing. I can do it without mentioning Winnie Cotterill, of course. She mustn't come in."

Walking down Kingsway he met a friend of his, a stockbroker whom he had not seen for some time, and invited him to a cup of tea at a neighbouring restaurant. In the course of conversation the broker remarked:

"I was saying something to my partner this morning not very complimentary to your profession, Crosby."

"What was that?"

"That the three classes of persons who make fools of themselves in finance are lawyers, parsons and old women."

"That's not kind," said Crosby with a laugh.

"It's true, though. We've had a big slump in the mining market to-day—'Virginian Reefs.' You haven't got any, I hope?"

"Not I!"

"You're lucky. They've gone down to three or four shillings—if you can get a bid. Now, look here, Crosby. I'm ready to bet you a new hat that you'll find a lot of old women and parsons and lawyers—not one of 'em knowing anything about mines—well hit over the job. I've bought myself, for a country vicar and the curate of a seaside town—and the biggest order I had for 'Virginian Reefs' came from a lawyer—a chap who won't take my advice."

"Who is he?"

"That's not a fair question. Staid old chap, living in a cathedral town—Frattenbury. I've had a frantic wire from him to sell out, but there aren't bidders for all the lot he holds. Well, he's wealthy, and can afford to drop a bit. Good-bye, old chap. I must be off."

Down in quiet, sleepy Frattenbury the superintendent received a wire that day from Sir James Perrivale:

E. G. started from Cape. Boat due Plymouth December 8.

"It's a waiting game, sir, then, for a few weeks," said Colson, to whom the superintendent showed the wire. "But I want a little time."

"Your week's up, and more," said the other. "Have you anything to tell the chief? He's getting restive."

"All right," said Colson. "I can tell him enough to keep him quiet—though I've several things to see to before I can satisfy him. I'm just off for a final visit to Marsh Quay. There's a question I want to ask that little blighter, Proctor, which has only just occurred to me."

"What's that?"

But Colson only shook his head, and started forth on his bicycle. The little man grinned at him when he was shown into his house at Marsh Quay.

"Come to arrest me again?"

"No, Mr. Proctor, I haven't. But I want to ask you something. Just carry your mind back to the inquest. Do you remember how that cigar band went round the jury?"

"Yes—perfectly. The Canon gave it to the coroner and he handed it to the jury. Nine of them had it before it came to me. I handed it over to the two others—across the table—and they returned it to the coroner."

"Yes—that's so. Then I suppose you recognised that band across the table—or somehow—before it got to you?"

"No, I didn't. It was only when I found it in my hand that I recognised it. Why do you ask?"

"Then why the dickens did you get ready to change it before you knew what it was?"

"*Change* it!" exclaimed Proctor. "What are you talking about? I never changed it!"

"What?" cried the detective, springing from his seat. "Do you mean to tell me you never——" He stopped suddenly. "Good Lord!" he said, sitting down in his chair again.

"What is it?" asked Proctor.

The detective thought rapidly.

"One of those two jurymen must have changed it," he said. "It was another band we found we had afterwards. For heaven's sake keep your mouth shut about it, Mr. Proctor."

"The jurymen. What—Bailey or Westall? They were the two. Why, my dear sir, Bailey is a most respectable man—so is Westall."

"It isn't a respectable man we're after, Mr. Proctor. It's a murderer. Remember, we even suspected *you*."

"But I can't believe——"

"Don't try, sir, don't try. Promise me you'll say nothing, now. It mustn't get out till we've investigated."

"Of course I'll say nothing. But you astound me."

"I'm astounded myself," said Colson, "though I really ought not to be. Good day, Mr. Proctor—mum's the word, remember."

He rushed back to Frattenbury and called at the Deanery. To his question, the maid informed him the Dean was abroad, and wouldn't be back till the first week in December. His language, as he came away, concerning clergy in general and Cathedral dignitaries in particular, was awful.

For two hours that evening he was closeted with the Chief Constable and the superintendent. All three men were exceedingly grave. Major Renshaw said at length:

"We must get all the evidence, Colson. It's an awful thing, if it's true. How about that stick!"

"I don't want to have to use it till we've proved the rest, sir. He might slip out of our hands on that alone."

"Also, there's Ezra Grice," said the superintendent.

"Yes—there's Ezra Grice," repeated the Chief Constable. "We'll wait for him."

As the weeks went by, Frattenbury and the newspapers forgot all about the murder. There were other matters for local gossip. People hinted that Francis Norwood was getting closer than ever with his cash. He demanded payments almost before he gave advice or transacted business. He sold a block of cottages belonging to him. And sundry creditors began to say they wished he was as ready to pay his bills as he was to be paid.

The Dean returned from his trip to the Riviera, and Colson called on him again. This time he came out of the Deanery evoking blessings on the heads of the clergy, instead of curses. There was another long conference between the three policemen—and their faces were graver than ever. Colson watched the shipping news anxiously, and one day took himself off to Plymouth, returning with a sallow-faced man who joined the trio at a further conference that evening—and it was very late when Colson took the stranger to his own house—where Mrs. Colson had a spare room ready for him.

"To-morrow, then," the Chief Constable had said, when Colson left, and Colson had repeated the words.

In the morning, the detective, who was carrying the stick he had found in the dinghy, met Canon Fittleworth. He stopped him.

"In confidence, sir," he said, "I shall have some news to tell you this evening—about your late cousin. Shall you be at home?"

"Indeed?" said the Canon, much interested. "Let me see—I'm alone in the house, and I've asked Mr. Norwood to dine with me—at half-past seven. Can you come about an hour earlier?"

A smile lingered on the detective's face, and he replied:

"Mr. Norwood might like to hear my news as well. Should I be intruding at—say nine o'clock?"

"Come, by all means."

"Thank you, sir—you won't mention this to Mr. Norwood?"

"If you don't want me to."

"I'd rather not, sir."

"Very well."

Colson, after this interview, did not pursue his way up the street. Instead, he retraced it to the police station.

"Better still, by and by," he remarked.

About eight o'clock he was walking up the street again, carrying the stick. He rang the bell of a quiet house in a quiet street. He was about five minutes inside that house, and then he went back to the police station, outwardly calm, but inwardly realising that this was the most intense moment of his life.

"It's perfectly true, sir," he said to the Chief Constable, holding out the walking-stick.

The Chief Constable sighed deeply.

"Very well," he said, "then there's nothing more to say about it."

A little before nine the three policemen, and the stranger staying in Colson's house, walked up the South Street together, and disappeared through the gateway half-way up the street into the quiet regions of the Cathedral Close.

"I ordered the taxi, sir," said Colson. "It will be all ready—outside the house—about half-past nine."

Major Renshaw nodded in silence. He was feeling the situation acutely.

CHAPTER XX.
Colson's "Imagination"

The maid who opened the door looked a little surprised when she found herself confronted with the four men.

"I think the Canon is engaged," she began, "he has someone——"

"Oh, he's expecting us—one of us, at least," said the Chief Constable. "I think he'll see us. Who is with him?"

"Mr. Norwood, sir."

"Very well, will you show us in, please? Except this gentleman—he will wait in the hall."

The Canon rose from his seat as the three policemen entered. Neither of them was in uniform. Major Renshaw, a punctilious man, wore evening dress. He always dressed for dinner.

Francis Norwood, seated in an arm-chair near the fire, also rose when he saw Major Renshaw. The Canon held out his hand in greeting.

"This is a surprise," he said; "I hardly expected——"

"You must forgive this intrusion, Canon," interrupted the Chief Constable. "Sergeant Colson mentioned that he was going to see you this evening, and we've taken the liberty of coming with him."

As he spoke he did not take the Canon's proffered hand. Instead, he bowed stiffly to him and Francis Norwood—who sat down once more. Indeed, the whole attitude of Major Renshaw savoured of officialism. The Canon apparently, noticed it. He stiffened slightly.

"Won't you sit down?" he asked.

The Chief Constable and the superintendent took the chairs he offered near the middle of the room. Colson, who had one hand behind his back, sat down in a chair near the door. When he had done so, he stooped to lay down his hat and stick, which he placed on the floor, behind a sofa.

"If I'm in the way, Fittleworth——" began Norwood.

"Not at all," broke in the Chief Constable; "don't let us disturb you."

Canon Fittleworth sat down again, wiped his pince-nez with his handkerchief, and adjusted them on his nose, and said, addressing the Major:

"Well now, Major, I don't know the purpose of your visit, but can only presume you have some news to impart. Is it about my late cousin?"

"Yes, it is—something you ought to know."

"In that case," said the Canon, "Mr. Norwood will be interested too."

Norwood nodded his head slightly, and said in his judicial manner:

"Naturally. My business with the unhappy affair ended, of course, with the verdict that was returned. But, as a private individual, I may be allowed some curiosity. Is there anything fresh, Major?"

"There is," said the Chief Constable, but addressing his remarks to the Canon as he spoke. "Detective-Sergeant Colson, as you know, has had the case in hand, and I'm going to ask you to let him tell you in his own way."

"Very well," said the Canon to Colson, "we shall be pleased to hear you."

Colson's face flushed slightly; he glanced round the room, and finally fixed his gaze on Canon Fittleworth. It was some moments before he began—the Chief Constable had even to say to him:

"Go on, Colson."

"Well, sir," said Colson, addressing the Canon, and never looking at anyone else, "this has not been an easy case at all, and I don't mind confessing that I've blundered considerably."

"You've done your best, sergeant, I'm sure. And no man can do more."

It was Norwood who spoke, but Colson took no notice of him. He only seemed to be aware of Canon Fittleworth's presence. He went on:

"My initial mistake, which led to others, was in taking it for granted that robbery was the motive for the murder—I allude to the diamonds. There were three persons who came under suspicion—there were ugly facts against each of them, especially as one of them was possessed of cigars of the same brand as those which you smoke, sir. And, in spite of the band being changed—or, rather, because of it—we felt quite sure that this individual was our man."

"What do you mean by the cigar band being changed?" asked Norwood.

But the detective never removed his eyes from the Canon.

"Yes—it was changed," he said. "I'll come to that later on. Well, as I was saying, these three men were cleared of all complicity with the crime. As for your cigars, Canon Fittleworth"—and he took a paper from his pocket—"I have a list here of all the persons to whom you gave any of those particular cigars, and I am satisfied that not one of them committed the murder, or knew anything about it."

"I'm very glad to hear that," said the Canon, a little uncomfortably, for the detective's fixed gaze was beginning to fascinate him strangely.

"It's true," went on Colson. "Well, the time came when I dismissed from my mind the idea that the robbery of the diamonds was the motive. I had to begin all over again. And now, Canon Fittleworth, I want to tell you how I imagine in my own mind that your cousin was done to death."

"Do you *know*?"

"I said 'imagine,' sir. Few people have ever witnessed the actual committal of a murder. Mr. Templeton, I think, was killed because he was a very foolish man. I would go so far as to say that he probably brought it on himself."

"But——" began the Canon.

"Please, sir," said the detective, holding up his hand, "let me tell my story in my own way. I want you to follow your cousin's movements in your mind from the time he left this house on the Saturday night."

"This is all imagination, I think you said?" asked Francis Norwood.

"This is all imagination, yes. But imagination often helps to reconstruct a crime. Well, sir, he left your house to keep an appointment."

"With whom?" asked the Canon.

"Ah," replied Colson, "there is no one to tell us that. There were no witnesses, we will suppose. Imagination, sir! He kept the appointment then. In Frattenbury. As this is imagination, we will call the person with whom he had an appointment 'Mr. Blank.' The end of this appointment was, that he and 'Mr. Blank' walked back together to Marsh Quay."

"Why?" asked the Canon.

"Probably—for I don't know—because your cousin asked him to go," said Colson. "I told you he was a very foolish man. I believe he had faced many dangers in the course of his life, but he was never in so much danger as when he took that walk back to his yacht. Shall I tell you the way the two men went? Yes? Imagination, remember, sir! Well, they didn't start along the well-lighted South Street. They went down the parallel street—only two lamps in it, sir—and hardly a soul there at that time of night. Then they went on to the Canal Basin—'Mr. Blank' had chosen the route—turned sharply to the right, crossed the main road, and took the field path leading to Marsh Quay.

"When they reached the shore your cousin pulled 'Mr. Blank' out to the yacht in his dinghy. 'Mr. Blank' was smoking a cigar at the time—or lighted it when he got on board the yacht."

"Why do you imagine that my cousin took him on board?"

"My fancy, sir, if you like. Let us say that there was something on board which your cousin had promised to show 'Mr. Blank'—or to give to him. And as soon as he produced it, 'Mr. Blank,' who, I think, must have armed himself with a weapon for the purpose, killed your cousin."

"But why——"

"Stop a moment, sir. Hear me out. 'Mr. Blank,' who had not noticed that the band had dropped off his cigar, very quickly relieved your cousin of any papers he had on him—we will imagine there was a reason for this—then he rowed ashore in the dinghy and did a very curious thing—it puzzled my imagination—at first. But I thought out a reason for it. He got hold of a canoe and took the dinghy back to the yacht again, making her fast, and finally paddled himself to shore in the canoe and walked back to Frattenbury, where he let himself into his house before, we will imagine, the theatrical performance at the Town Hall was quite over. Well, sir, *that's* my theory of how your cousin was murdered."

He paused. The Chief Constable and the superintendent sat like two statues. Francis Norwood leaned a little forward in his chair, and remarked, with a touch of sarcasm:

"A very lucid story, sergeant. I hope you may be successful in tracking down this 'Mr. Blank.'"

But, again ignoring the coroner, Colson went on—to the Canon: "What do you think of it, sir?"

"I don't know what to think. It's so very strange. But, to confine ourselves to your definition, can you imagine the motive?"

"Yes, sir," replied Colson, very quietly. "I think I can."

"What was it?"

"Something that the law would call by a very ugly name—'blackmail.' That's what I think, sir."

"Blackmail!—this 'Mr. Blank'?"

"No, sir. Mr. Templeton!"

"My cousin a blackmailer!" exclaimed Canon Fittleworth. "Preposterous!"

"I said that's what the law would call him, sir. Please—let me go on. I haven't quite finished. Let me imagine something further."

For the first time since he had begun to speak, he took his eyes off the Canon, and gave a rapid glance at Superintendent Norton. Then he looked at the Canon again.

"What I am about to imagine now," he said slowly, "is first that the Dean gave 'Mr. Blank' one of the Canon's cigars, secondly that 'Mr. Blank' was a left-handed man, and thirdly that he made one fatal mistake—he left his walking-stick in the dinghy—and this is it!"

He lifted the walking-stick, suddenly, from behind the sofa and held it out to the Canon. Then he turned in a flash, and sprang across the room.

"Mr. Norwood, I arrest you for the murder of Reginald Templeton."

There was a flash of steel and a click. Francis Norwood, who had risen to his feet when Colson had darted towards him, stood there, the handcuffs on his wrist.

"Damn you!" he exclaimed, for once losing his frigidity. "What do you mean? That isn't my stick. I had one like it, it is true, but I know that isn't mine—I——"

"Norwood," broke in the Chief Constable sternly, "it is my duty to warn you that anything you say will be taken down and may be given in evidence."

"It *is* your stick," said Colson gravely. "Your housekeeper recognised it this evening. I've had it from the first. The one you removed from the dinghy the next night was a dummy. I put it there."

The astonished Canon looked from one to the other, and exclaimed to Major Renshaw:

"Is this—is this extraordinary action countenanced by *you*, Major?"

"I fear it is, Canon," replied Major Renshaw. "Knowing what we do—and there is a great deal more—I have no option in the matter."

"But this is terrible—terrible!"

Francis Norwood, still deadly pale, recovered a little from the shock.

"This is unpardonable of you, Major Renshaw. I demand an explanation."

"Colson will give you one, Mr. Norwood. But I fear it will not help you."

He nodded to the detective, who opened the door. A thin, white-faced, emaciated man came into the room. Norwood regarded him with horror.

"Ezra Grice!" he exclaimed in a low voice. "I—I thought he was dead!"

"I know you did," said Colson, "or you wouldn't have been so eager to help with that advertisement. Shall I ask Grice to tell his story?"

"No—no," said the lawyer. "No—yes—I don't care if he does. It's all a pack of lies, and he can't prove anything."

"It doesn't matter whether he can or not," said Colson. "I haven't arrested you because of something you did twenty years ago. You are charged with murder—not embezzlement. May I go on, sir?" he asked the Chief Constable.

"It is irregular, Colson," said the Major stiffly.

"I should very much like to know more," put in the bewildered Canon. "I think I have a right to ask. You've arrested one of my friends in my own house—charged with the murder of my cousin.

Norwood," and he went up to the lawyer, "won't you tell me you didn't do this awful thing? I can't believe it!"

"You've heard what Major Renshaw said," replied Norwood. "Anything I say may incriminate me. I have no desire to discuss the matter further at this point."

"We owe you a further explanation, Canon, as you say," remarked the Chief Constable, "and with your permission, Colson shall remain—and Mr. Grice."

The Canon nodded.

"Thank you," he said. "They may stay."

"Come!" said the superintendent. Between him and the Chief Constable the coroner walked out of the room, and a motor was heard a few moments later. Canon Fittleworth sat down and buried his head in his hands. Presently he said:

"I'm thankful my wife and daughter are not at home."

"It wouldn't have happened here, sir, if they had been, I assure you. You told me, you know, that you were alone."

The Canon nodded.

"Go on," he said. "I want to hear it all—poor Reginald!"

"It's a long story, sir, but I'll try to make it as short as possible. The first idea that set me on the right track was that the murderer was a left-handed man. I found out that Mr. Templeton did not walk with a stick—I mean, didn't put the point to the ground. There were square tracks of the stick's ferrule on the path to Marsh Quay, on the left side as you go out."

"But what made you suspect the stick had anything to do with it?"

Colson told him how the dummy one had been removed on the night after the murder, and then went on.

"I was on the look-out for a left-handed man, and one day I saw Mr. Norwood draw a cork from a bottle. He held the bottle with his right hand and drew it with his left. It seemed preposterous, but when I noticed him another day walking down the street with a stick in his left hand it set me thinking. I got the report of the inquest, and studied it carefully, noting all the coroner's questions. And it seemed to me that he was particularly anxious to find out whether anyone had an idea as to your cousin's appointment. Also, when Jim Webb mentioned that he had read the address on the letter to you, he questioned him narrowly as to whether he had read any other addresses. Then he must have felt secure until you produced that cigar band. I thought for a long time that Proctor had changed it, but when I found he hadn't, I knew it could only have been the coroner himself."

"Why?"

"There were several old bands off cigars that had been smoked by Grayson, lying in the grate. Don't you remember that the coroner dropped some papers in the grate, and stooped down to get them? So did Proctor. That's why I suspected him first. Afterwards I saw it all. While that cigar band was passing round the jury, the coroner picked up one from the grate and changed it. Clever! But it was a foolish thing to do, as it turned out.

"You told me you gave a dozen of your cigars to the Dean. He remembered that when Norwood was dining with him afterwards—just a day or two before the murder—he smoked one of them, and liked it so much that the Dean gave him a couple, which he put in his case.

"Well, in Norwood's hall, when I went to see him one day, I noticed several queer photographs and old weapons—three or four small daggers among them—hanging on the wall. Then Mr. Crosby was a great help; he put me on the track of finding Ezra Grice. There was a letter partly blotted on Mr. Templeton's blotting-pad that gave us the clue. And Mr. Crosby also found out the beginning of the whole story, and accidentally discovered that the coroner was speculating heavily—and that had a lot to do with things. He wanted money."

"Dear me," said the Canon. "I imagined him to be a wealthy man."

"So did most people, sir, but after what we heard we made inquiries, and found out a lot about him. And I assure you that even if I hadn't arrested him to-night, he'd very soon have been in the bankruptcy court."

"You astonish me."

"It's true, sir. Now, when our friend Ezra Grice here arrived from South Africa, he solved the rest of the mystery. We have his sworn statement. Will you tell the Canon, Mr. Grice?"

Grice, who had not spoken hitherto, said:

"Yes, I will. Where shall I begin?"

"At the beginning—twenty years ago."

"You'll find it a strange story, sir," said Colson. "And it will explain why I said the law would have called your cousin a blackmailer."

CHAPTER XXI.
Final Solution of the Problem

It was an extraordinary story that Ezra Grice had to tell. Briefly, the first part of it amounted to this. Twenty years ago he had been clerk in Francis Norwood's office. Norwood, at that time, had a partner, a young married man named Forbes. Forbes was tried on a charge of embezzlement, and Grice was a witness for the prosecution. But Grice was deeply involved himself. Addicted to betting, he had helped himself to the firm's money—falsifying accounts.

Just before the trial commenced he made a discovery—a discovery that would have proved Forbes an innocent man. And the discovery he made was that Norwood himself, who had been speculating heavily, had embezzled the money from two clients—and not Forbes at all. Knowing this, he went into Norwood's private office and accused him of the crime.

But Norwood turned the tables on him. To Grice's horror, he calmly produced proofs of the clerk's defalcations, and threatened to give him in charge instantly.

"And who is going to believe you *then*?" he asked calmly. "Do you think they'll take the word of a thief against mine?"

Grice, who had no proofs in his possession at the time, but had only arrived at his conclusions by a study of accounts and documents passing through his hands, was staggered. He felt he had matched himself unwisely against the astute lawyer—who was quick to see this.

"Very well," Norwood had said, "you can take your choice. Either I send for a policeman at once, or you withdraw what you say, and give your evidence to-morrow. Which is it to be? I give you five minutes to decide."

Ezra Grice decided before the five minutes were up. He caved in, abjectly. As soon as the trial was over, and Forbes was sentenced, Norwood coolly told him that unless he left Frattenbury at once and never returned, he would prosecute him for theft.

"And if I say what I know?" asked Grice.

"They won't believe you if you do; and if they do believe you, then you'll be prosecuted for perjury as well."

Again the wretched clerk gave in. But before he left the office that very day he made a fresh discovery—a paper which Norwood had left out of his safe that absolutely incriminated him. He was half inclined to make use of this paper and have his revenge on the wily lawyer, but fear got the better of him. However, when he left Frattenbury the next day he took this paper with him and kept it carefully.

He went out to South Africa and led a roving life for years keeping honest all the time. He had had one great fright, and that was enough for him. He always kept the incriminating paper; he was in dread that perhaps one day his crime might follow him, and he looked upon it as a weapon of defence in case he ever met Norwood again. Finally, as Sir James Perrivale had said, he joined Reginald Templeton in an exploration in the interior.

"It was a long time," he went on to the Canon, "before I told Mr. Templeton my story—and he was the only man to whom I ever told it before the police took it down here. I happened to mention Frattenbury one day, and he questioned me, but I didn't let him know anything then. However, I saw he knew something about the Forbes case and was interested in it.

"Then he saved my life. I got to like him. He was a queer man, but very kind to me always. I shall never forget how he stood by me on that awful journey before we struck Sir James Perrivale's camp. My arm was broken and I was down with fever. He'd help to carry the stretcher himself—miles at a time.

"I asked him point-blank one day if he was interested in Forbes. He only answered 'Yes.' Then I said, 'Would it be any use to you to know he was innocent of that charge?' I shan't forget what he said. He questioned me eagerly and I told him all about it. Then he said, 'Thank God for this, Grice. Forbes died long ago; but he's left a daughter—and, by God, that scoundrel Norwood shall make it up to her!'

"He made me promise I'd go back to England with him—if we ever came through—and help him expose Norwood—or, rather, he said he was not going to expose him—he'd got a better card to play than that. But it seemed that I wasn't going to get back to England.

They all thought me dying when we got to the camp. Mr. Templeton had to go on, but before he left he wrote down my statement which I signed before witnesses, and asked me to give him that paper I had on me. Of course I did, and then he told me what he was going to do. I can hear him saying it now.

" 'You'll have your revenge on Norwood,' he said. 'And it's a revenge that will touch him to the quick on his sorest point. Forbes is dead, and we can't help him. And his wife is dead. But there's her daughter. If I were to give Norwood into the hands of the law there'd be no recompense for *her*. But, by God, there *shall* be! As soon as I get back to the old country I shall write to Norwood, tell him what I know, and offer him choice between exposure and ten thousand pounds.' "

"That is where the blackmail comes in, sir," interposed Colson quietly. "And I don't know that I wouldn't justify it—but the law wouldn't."

"Go on, please," said the Canon to Grice.

"Well, sir, he went on to say that if he got this sum out of Norwood he should settle it on Forbes's daughter—not telling her where it came from, and not letting her know about her father. He said she was only a child at the time—well, I knew that; I've often seen her here—and that she had been brought up in ignorance of her father's crime."

"I think I know who she was," murmured the Canon. "That accounts for those strange impressions of having been here before—and recognising Norwood. Yes?"

Ezra Grice finished the story, and the detective took up the threads.

"Now do you see, sir?" he asked. "Mr. Templeton evidently carried out his threat and wrote to Norwood on his return. Then he made an appointment with him. He wrote saying he was prepared to hand over Grice's confession and proofs in exchange for the money. Norwood must have been in a terrible dilemma. He must get those proofs in any case; it would mean utter ruin to him if he was once exposed. But he hadn't the money to buy them. Whether or not he meant to bluff your cousin remains to be seen. Anyhow, he made the appointment, and sent his domestics to the performance at the

Town Hall that night—I've found out that—in order to be alone when Templeton called."

"But why go back to Marsh Quay with him?" asked the Canon.

"Don't you see, sir? I think we can guess. Templeton hadn't got the confession and proofs on him. He made a mistake by being too careful. You told us he said he was very likely going to spend a few nights here. Very well. That particular night he wasn't prepared to hand them over. The coroner had probably not committed himself, even by a typewritten, unsigned letter. And he knew he hadn't the money."

"What *did* he do, then?" asked the Canon.

"Probably pretended that he *had* got it, and induced Templeton to give him the proofs that night. By this time he had made up his mind that he *must* have them—in any case. And I think he took that dagger, or whatever it was, with him—ready to take the biggest risk of all. Which we know he did!"

Canon Fittleworth sat for a few minutes in silence. Then he said:

"Thank you, Sergeant Colson, and thank you also, Mr. Grice. The whole affair has been terrible—very terrible. I want time to think it over. I must say, however, Colson, that you are a very clever man to have found out all this."

"Thank you, sir. I did my best. And someone helped me very much. Good night, sir. I'm very sorry all this has happened."

Colson and Ezra Grice went out, leaving the Canon seated in his chair gazing at the fire, his mind greatly agitated.

At the police station that night Norwood asked to be provided with writing materials. They did so.

He smiled sardonically while they searched him and took away a penknife and a pair of pocket nail-scissors.

But in the morning they found him hanging to the bar of the window—they have out-of-date cells in Frattenbury—his braces substituted for the rope that he would have eventually earned. And on the table was a characteristic document:

I am anxious to assist my successor, though I fancy he will have no trouble in persuading the jury as to the verdict. I am a ruined man, with no more use for the world. Sergeant Colson's "imagination" is fairly correct. I will only add that I persuaded Templeton I had the money. He had demanded cash. I showed him what appeared to be a roll of notes—tissue-paper with some genuine ones at the top. I also told him that unless he gave me what Ezra Grice has probably described that night, I should abscond—with the ten thousand pounds on me. He made a mistake in not bringing what he had for sale—he was too cautious. It was the dagger hanging in my hall when I put my coat on that suggested I might have to take a desperate step. I took it with me. Templeton produced what I wanted from the locker. Then he was fool enough to examine the roll of notes I had laid on the table. That was the end of it. I took the contents of his pockets to make sure in case he had anything with my name on it. I desire to say that I regret what I did, but I was desperate that night. That is all.

"Mr. Crosby," said the Canon the following day—the lawyer had come down to Frattenbury on receipt of a wire from the police—"I want to ask you something."

"What is it?"

"This girl, Winifred Cotterill—or Forbes, as we must call her now. If there had been a trial, I suppose everything would have come out?"

"About her father? Certainly. Ezra Grice would have given evidence, and the girl must have guessed."

"I thought so. As it is, however, she has never heard about her father's sufferings. Poor fellow, what he must have gone through! The matter, you tell me, rests in your hands. What are you going to do about it? Shall you tell her the whole story?"

The lawyer thought for a minute or two, and replied shortly:

"I don't know, Canon Fittleworth. That is a question I shall have to consider. I haven't made up my mind yet."

THE END

Printed in Great Britain
by Amazon